DISNEY

HIGH SCHOOL MUSICAL 2

Book of the Film
Adapted by N.B. Grace

Based on "High School Musical 2," Written by Peter Barsocchini

Based on Characters Created by Peter Barsocchini

PaRRagon

Bath · New York · Singapore · Hong Kong · Cologne · Delhi · Melbourne

This is a Parragon book

This edition published in 2008
Parragon
Queen Street House
4 Queen Street
Bath, BA1 1HE, UK

Copyright © 2007 Disney Enterprises, Inc.

ISBN 978-1-4075-3130-4
Printed in UK

DISNEY

HIGH SCHOOL MUSICAL 2

CHAPTER ONE

The halls of East High School were eerily quiet. The auditorium was deserted. Not one sound echoed inside the cavernous cafeteria. In the gym, a lone caretaker mopped the floor. No one was rushing up the stairs, no one was running down the hall. In fact, the only sound that could be heard was Ms Darbus talking to her tutor group.

But no one, of course, was listening. Troy Bolton gazed at the wall clock as the minute hand jumped to 2:58 p.m. He glanced over at

Gabriella Montez, who smiled back. Only two minutes until they were free!

Ms Darbus seemed completely unaware of the fact that she didn't have everyone's rapt attention. "Learning is never seasonal, so do allow the shimmering light of summer to refresh and illuminate your fertile young minds," she said.

Sharpay Evans frowned at the ticking clock while her brother, Ryan Evans, gazed absently out of the window at cloud formations. Chad Danforth struggled to keep his eyes open as he did a silent countdown to 3 p.m. in his head. Zeke Baylor seemed to be studying – but he had hidden *How to Bake the Perfect Muffin* inside his advanced algebra textbook and was actually reading about batter. Martha Cox's feet were dancing with impatience under her desk. Taylor McKessie sat with her hands folded on her desk, looking like the perfect student, even though she was as anxious as any of them for the bell to ring. And Jason Cross . . . Jason was actually taking notes on what Ms Darbus was saying!

2

"Your future greets you with its magic mirror, reflecting each golden moment, each emboldened choice," Ms Darbus went on. "So use these incipient summer days and weeks wisely and well . . ."

Troy leaned over to whisper to Chad, "Ms Darbus has snapped her cap."

Chad opened his eyes wide in surprise. "Dude," he said, "you're actually *listening*?"

Sharpay began tapping her fingers on her desk to the rhythm of the second hand. After a few seconds, she tapped even faster, willing the time to speed by, and turned to her brother. "Ryan, this semester of disappointment and humiliation now comes to a screeching halt, and the future begins," she whispered. "And that means–"

But Ryan wasn't listening. He was still staring out of the window.

"Ryan!" she snapped.

"Is it me," he asked dreamily, "or do those clouds look like Jessica Simpson?"

As the students fidgeted in their seats, the sound of ticking seemed to get even louder, drowning out Ms Darbus's voice . . .

And the clock on the wall seemed to get bigger and bigger as everyone stared at it longingly . . .

"Summers have passed fleetingly since I was your age," Ms Darbus went on wistfully. "Yet I recall them with poignant clarity, so . . ."

Jason raised his hand.

"Yes, Jason?" Ms Darbus said.

"What's your favourite summer memory, Ms Darbus?" Jason asked.

The entire class groaned. What was Jason *thinking*?!

But Ms Darbus was happy to answer him. "Ah, yes, the Ashland Shakespeare Festival of '88 leaps fondly to mind. In fact . . ."

Claaannnggg! Just in the nick of time, the bell rang . . . and the whole school erupted in cheers!

Classroom doors were flung open and students poured into the halls. It was time to say goodbye to school and hello to summer!

As Troy, Chad, Zeke and Jason walked together towards their lockers, Troy said, "Dudes, when hoops camp is done, I've got to make bank. I keep hearing my parents talk about what college is going to cost."

"Yeah, my folks will match whatever I make this summer, but first I've got to get hired," Zeke said.

"Me, too," Chad agreed. "I'm saving for a car . . ." He nodded towards Taylor, who was standing across the hall. ". . . so I can take that girl on a proper date." He expertly spun the basketball he was carrying. "Unfortunately, this is my only job skill."

His friends nodded ruefully. Getting a summer job wasn't going to be easy, especially since they were in high school. Still, nothing could dampen the excitement of the last day of school!

Talking and laughing, everyone headed for the front doors . . . but not without a few last goodbye rituals, like the signing of yearbooks.

Sharpay stood by her trademark pink locker

and signed her name with a grand flourish. She occasionally flashed a smile at the student photographer who was snapping away with his camera, recording this celebrity moment for posterity.

Gabriella paused to watch what passed for a media frenzy in the halls of East High. Sharpay glanced at her and said, "I understand you've moved every summer for the past five years. I'd hate to think that today is . . ." She gave Gabriella a hopeful smile. ". . . *goodbye?*"

Gabriella smiled back, but it was because she was so happy knowing that all the years of moving from town to town had come to an end. "No worries. My mum promised I'm here until graduation next year," Gabriella answered cheerfully.

Sharpay's face fell. "Bless mum's little heart," she said insincerely.

Gabriella could feel the tension. She decided that this was the perfect moment to mend fences. Or at least try to keep them from completely falling apart.

"Sharpay, we got off to a rough start, but you came through," she said. "You helped me with the winter musical."

"I did?" Sharpay couldn't believe what she was hearing. When had she helped Gabriella? And how? And how could she make sure she never made such a mistake again?

Gabriella nodded. "Those breathing exercises . . ." She took a deep breath, held it for a moment, then let it out slowly, demonstrating what Sharpay had taught her.

"Delighted to assist a fellow Wildcat," Sharpay said in a tone that made clear she bitterly regretted offering *any* advice to Gabriella Montez. With effort, she added, "And, actually, I appreciated the opportunity to rest my voice for the spring musical."

"In which you were excellent," Gabriella said.

"So they say . . ." Sharpay said, gratified. Always ready to relive a triumph, she pulled a copy of the school newspaper from her locker. A huge photo of her filled most of the front page under a headline that read: SHARPAY SOARS.

"The second show on the third Friday wasn't everything it might have been," she said, "but the media is so easily impressed."

Then she threw the newspaper back in her locker, where it landed on top of 50 other copies. Gabriella grinned and moved on to her own locker. At the other end of the hall, Troy, Chad, Zeke and Jason were still talking about summer jobs, and now Taylor, Kelsi Nielsen and Martha had joined in the conversation.

"Gabriella and I have had five job interviews, but we keep getting beat out by college kids," Taylor said.

"Same here," Martha sighed. "Guess I'm back in the babysitting business. Kelsi, what are you planning to do this summer?"

Kelsi looked up at Martha, who was a little taller. "Grow," she said wryly. She added the obvious, "Write music." Then she glanced up at Taylor, who was a *lot* taller than her, shook her head and said again, "Grow."

Gabriella had almost finished cleaning out her locker when Troy sneaked up behind her and wrapped his arms around her in a hug.

"Your summer activities consultant has arrived," he said in a teasing voice.

Startled, she looked around, and he grinned at her. "Me! After basketball camp, we'll see movies, download music, a little karaoke, and I'm definitely teaching you a twisted flip on the skateboard."

She laughed. "I have Red Cross training, so I can patch myself up afterwards."

Sharpay was standing close enough to over-hear their teasing, and she rolled her eyes.

"Hey, worse comes to worst, we just chill," Troy said. "As long as we spend summer together, it's all good."

Gabriella looked up at him. "Promise?"

He nodded as he pulled a necklace from his pocket and handed it to her. "Here's my promise."

Gabriella's eyes widened with surprise as she

saw the 'T' hanging from the necklace. Across the hall, Taylor and Chad noticed this moment – and Chad, of course, had to make a joke. He pretended to offer her his basketball as a present, but she just gave him a withering look and turned back to see what would happen next.

For a moment, she thought Troy was actually going to kiss Gabriella. Until, that is, a couple of starry-eyed freshmen girls came squealing up to ask him to sign their yearbooks.

As he agreeably autographed their books, Sharpay turned to Ryan. ". . . going to movies, listening to music . . . and, golly, Troy, I have Red Cross training so you can teach me skateboarding," she said in a falsely sweet voice, mimicking what she had overheard. Then, in her own voice, she added, "What she really needs is new product for her wayward hair."

She saw Kelsi standing at her locker, watching the other Wildcats wistfully. "Cheer up, Kelsi, I have a summer job for you," Sharpay said. "Our rehearsal pianist is evidently moving."

"Or hiding," Kelsi said under her breath.

Sharpay's eyes narrowed. "Pardon?"

Ryan saw the warning signs of a real snit coming on, and he quickly jumped in. "Relax, Sharpay. It's summer. You get to do whatever you want. Everything changes."

At Ryan's words, Sharpay's head snapped around again, this time to give her brother that look of intense focus and concentration that always made him so nervous.

"What did I say?" he squeaked.

"You're so right, Ryan," she said. "After what I've been through this semester, I deserve a special summer."

Troy, Gabriella, Chad, Taylor and the rest of their crew walked past, headed for the front doors. Sharpay watched them go, thinking hard.

"Ryan, who is the absolute primo boy at East High?" she asked.

Ryan rolled his eyes at the utter obviousness of the answer. "I think Troy Bolton has locked up that category, don't you?"

"And East High's primo girl?" she went on.

Ryan glanced warily at Gabriella.

"Just answer the question!" Sharpay snapped.

"Gosh, let me think," Ryan said as sarcastically as he dared. "You?"

Sharpay nodded with immense self-satisfaction. "Troy . . . Sharpay. Sharpay . . . Troy," she said musingly. "It just makes sense."

"Evidently not to Troy," Ryan pointed out.

But Sharpay wasn't listening to him. She was focusing on the delicious plot that was beginning to form in her brain. "But it's summer, Ryan," she said, smiling. "Everything changes."

A few feet away, Kelsi took some sheet music from her locker and looked at Sharpay thoughtfully. What, she wondered, was the diva of East High up to now? Then she glanced down the hall and watched as the Wildcats burst out through the front doors into summer . . . and freedom!

CHAPTER TWO

Two weeks later, Troy, Jason, Zeke and Chad were back from basketball camp – but that didn't mean they weren't still playing hoops every second they could. One evening, they piled into the Boltons' kitchen after their workout.

Troy's father, Coach Bolton, followed them, throwing them bottles of water. "What I saw out there just now looks very, very strong, guys," he said. "Camp really stepped up your game."

Chad yelled, "What team?"

They yelled back, "Wildcats!"

Just then, the phone rang. Troy answered it. As he walked away from the guys, Chad said, "Uh-oh, girlfriend alert."

The other guys laughed, but Troy was already in the next room. The caller wasn't Gabriella. It was a man Troy had never met before – but who seemed to know an awful lot about him.

"This is Thomas Fulton over at Lava Springs," the man said. "I understand you've been looking for summer work?"

"Hey, Troy, does Gabriella still remember your name, or did she karaoke with someone new on vacation?" Zeke called out from the kitchen.

As the guys cracked up, Troy waved at them to be quiet. "That sounds fantastic, Mr Fulton," he said. "But how did you get my name?"

"We've always had a student summer work programme here at Lava Springs," he said smoothly. After a second, he added, "Go Wildcats."

Okay, Troy thought, fair enough. But if it was a student summer work programme, maybe there was a way he could make this sudden opportunity into something even more fun . . .

"Here's the thing," he said. "I know this really great girl . . . I mean, *student* . . . straight As, *quintuple* straight As, and she's looking for a job, too, and it'd be so amazingly perfect if . . ."

He kept talking, pacing around the room as he tried to sell Mr Fulton his really great idea.

"Man, he's really working someone," Chad said.

"It can't be Gabriella," his father said. "When she calls, he just blushes." He looked at the guys, catching himself. "I never said that."

Finally, Troy was done. He hung up the phone looking pleased.

"What's up, dog?" Chad asked.

"Up?" Troy said with a grin. "What? Nothing."

He slapped the basketball out of Chad's hands and dribbled it around the kitchen, causing immediate chaos as everyone went after him.

"Hey, not in the house!" his dad yelled. "Troy's mother will be home in a minute, then we're all dead!"

They immediately calmed down.

"I'll tell you what, though," he added, "you stick together this summer, work on the game, and we're talking back-to-back championships next fall."

"Bet on it," Troy said with confidence.

His friends looked at him, curious. They could tell he had something up his sleeve. But what?

His dad took advantage of their momentary distraction to steal the ball. Instantly, the kitchen was again in an uproar, until the ball was snatched from mid-air and everyone turned to see . . .

. . . Troy's mum, holding the basketball and giving them her Mum Look. "Do you think we can all redirect this energy towards carrying in the groceries?" she asked calmly.

"Yes, Mrs Bolton," everyone said – even Coach Bolton.

The Lava Springs Country Club was heaven on Earth – if you were a member. The clubhouse gleamed with brand-new paint. Tanned, happy people sprawled on chairs underneath the beach umbrellas that surrounded the swimming pool. On the patio, members enjoyed their lunch in the warm sunshine of a beautiful summer day.

It was the perfect day . . . until a convertible with a number plate that read FABULOUS rolled through the front gates. It purred up the driveway to the portico. A valet rushed forward to greet the driver . . . none other than Sharpay.

"Miss Evans, Mr Evans – looking very sharp this summer," the valet said.

In the passenger seat, Ryan tipped his stylish hat in greeting.

"Thank you, David," Sharpay said, with just the right combination of reserve and warmth. "Can you find some shade for our car?"

Before the valet could answer, another voice said, "Even if we have to plant a tree, Miss Evans." Mr Fulton stepped forward and added smoothly, "I trust that your vacation was satisfactory?"

Sharpay shrugged. "New York, for shopping and Broadway shows. Seven days, eight shows, 11 new pairs of shoes. However, it's good to be . . ."

She looked around and sighed with satisfaction. ". . . home."

She and Ryan got out of the car and walked with Mr Fulton towards the clubhouse. Sharpay waved graciously to other club members and staff as she proceeded up the drive. A warm glow filled her heart as everyone responded to her greetings. Now I know how the Queen of England feels when she returns to Buckingham Palace, she thought.

Then something caught her eye. "Is it possible to get more colour in these gardens?" she asked. "I'm thinking yellows and blues."

Mr Fulton nodded quickly. "Lovely." He snapped his fingers at a gardener and pointed to the flowerbed.

Sharpay smiled happily. It was so nice to be in a place where her slightest suggestion was treated as an order to be obeyed! If only the rest of the world operated like the Lava Springs Country Club, she thought.

As she and Ryan swept into the lobby, Sharpay caught sight of a display cabinet. There was her father's photo, with a nameplate that said Club Founder and President. There was her mother's photo, with a placard that read Director of Membership Committee.

Next to these sat gleaming trophies celebrating the Evans' triumphs in swimming, diving, tennis, golf and ballroom dancing competitions that had been held at the country club.

Her gaze moved on to a poster advertising the club's next big social event: LAVA SPRINGS' ANNUAL MIDSUMMER NIGHT'S STAR DAZZLE TALENT SHOW! MAKE RESERVATIONS NOW!

Mr Fulton pointed to a stack of programmes lying on a reception table. "This year we embossed the flyers for the show."

"Inspired," Sharpay replied. She pulled out a marker and began autographing the flyers. "I plan to limit member talent auditions to 30 seconds each. Amateur performers are very . . ."

"Draining?" Mr Fulton filled in helpfully. "Understood."

"And should I . . ." She paused and quickly

included Ryan in her statement. ". . . *we* be so fortunate as to win the Star Dazzle award again . . ."

"We're planning to widen the trophy case," Mr Fulton said. "I have sketches in my office."

She beamed at him. Mr Fulton was truly a treasure! "You are *so* efficient," she cooed.

This summer was shaping up to be the best one ever, she thought. So far, everything was going according to plan. She just had one other little matter to take care of. "The staffing matter we discussed . . . ?" she whispered to Mr Fulton. "Handled, with discretion," he assured her.

"How . . . fabulous," she replied. Then she headed off to the locker room. Time to put the next phase of Operation Perfect Summer into motion.

CHAPTER THREE

A few minutes later, Sharpay emerged from the locker room wearing a gorgeous swimsuit, a cute cover-up and a dramatic sun hat. She carried a brightly coloured parasol and a shoulder bag stuffed with sunscreen, mobile phone, make-up, flip-flops and magazines.

She heard breathless greetings and turned to see three girls named Jackie, Lea and Emma rushing over. They seemed thrilled to have spotted her.

A voice behind Sharpay said, "Your chaise in its usual spot, Miss Evans?" She turned to see a pool attendant hovering nearby.

"Wonderful, Javier," she said. "Emma and Jackie west of me, Lea east. And you'll be a prince to angle our chaises on the hour, as the sun moves."

He smiled. "Thanks to the kind words from your mother last season, I've been promoted, but I'll see to it that the new lifeguard is fully briefed on your requirements," he assured her.

Imagining herself a queen settling on her throne, Sharpay sat down. Her attendants – she caught herself – her *girlfriends* gathered around her.

"So what's the theme of the summer talent show, Sharpay?" Emma asked eagerly.

Sharpay paused dramatically, then said one simple word: "Redemption."

The girls exchanged confused glances, then Lea spoke for all of them. "Huh?"

Sharpay sighed. How could she explain what the last year had been like?

She settled for saying, "It was a very . . . trying . . . year, ladies." After a moment, she gathered her strength and went on. "My drama department was invaded by outsiders – singers coming out of the chemistry lab and locker room."

"It's over, Sharpay," Ryan said. He had emerged from the changing room in time to overhear the last of her complaints. "It's summer, remember? We've got the pool and the entire club, and the whole summer to enjoy it."

"And the spa has been redone," Emma pointed out.

"There's an avocado facial and seaweed body scrub on the menu," Jackie added.

"It's all too perfect," Lea sighed happily.

"Oh, really?" Sharpay said. Nothing was ever *completely* perfect, after all. She frowned at her glass, then raised it in the air to get the attention of a waiter. "More ice, please."

If not completely perfect, life at the Lava Springs Country Club was definitely fabulous! And, the girls noticed, it had just got better. A cute guy was heading their way. They adjusted their sunglasses to get a better look. When they saw who it was, they exchanged surprised glances . . . everyone but Sharpay, that is.

The boy was none other than Troy Bolton, carrying a tray of drinks to the poolside. Sharpay smiled to herself . . . until she spotted Chad, Jason and Zeke being led towards the pool area by Mr Fulton. Her smile disappeared. What was going on here?

And Troy didn't even notice her! Sharpay turned to follow his gaze – and saw Gabriella, looking beautiful in a lifeguard swimsuit, her hair flowing in the breeze!

Sharpay's mouth dropped open. She stood and took a couple of uncertain steps backwards. Everywhere she looked, she saw nothing but Wildcats! It was all just . . . TOO . . . MUCH! Stunned, she took another step back and . . . *SPLASH!!!*

Sharpay floundered in the water, spluttering, hoping that this was just a terrible dream and that any minute now she would wake up–

An arm grabbed her around the neck and pulled her to the edge of the pool. Gasping,

Sharpay turned to see Gabriella, who had dived into the water when she saw Sharpay struggling.

"What are you DOING HERE?!" Sharpay yelled.

"I'm the new lifeguard," Gabriella explained.

Troy looked confused. "Are *you* a member here?" he asked Sharpay.

Sharpay gasped. Was *she* a member? Was she a *member*? If Lava Springs Country Club had a royal family, she would be the princess! And right now, she was one very angry princess!

"I asked you to hire *Troy Bolton*, not the entire East High student body!" Sharpay screamed. She had Mr Fulton pinned against the wall. Ryan was at her side, looking suitably outraged.

"Troy Bolton was insistent that Miss Montez have a job," Mr Fulton said evenly. "She's Red Cross certified, you know."

"That's already been clearly pointed out to me!" Sharpay yelled. She wasn't sure she would *ever* get over the humiliation of being rescued by Gabriella.

"And Troy was most persuasive on behalf of his team-mates," Mr Fulton continued. "Something about working together, winning together."

Sharpay rolled her eyes. "Rah-rah, sis-boom-bah."

"You told me whatever it takes to hire Troy Bolton," the manager reminded her. "Well, this is what it took."

"Why didn't you warn me about the rest of them?" she wailed.

Mr Fulton stiffened. "I did discuss the matter with the Lava Springs board, of course."

"The board . . ." Ryan looked from Mr Fulton to his sister, his mouth dropping open as the truth slowly dawned. "You mean, our . . ."

"*Mother*!" Sharpay screamed.

It didn't take long to track Mrs Evans down. She was in her yoga class, doing the downward-dog position. Sharpay and Ryan took up the position themselves in order to talk to her.

"I thought it would be a lovely surprise, my

darlings," Mrs Evans said. "When Mr Fulton informed me that Troy Bolton wanted more Wildcats here, I thought, how brilliant!"

"Brilliant?" Sharpay was outraged.

Her mother twisted into another position. Sharpay and Ryan did the same.

"Think about the future, kitten," Mrs Evans said. "These are chums, not the fuddy-duddy Lava Springs members."

Sharpay reminded herself that it was bad manners to scream in the middle of a yoga class. "These are not my *chums*!" she said as loudly as she dared. "They'll steal my summer show!"

Her mother smiled serenely (yoga helped her a great deal when it came to dealing with Sharpay). "And what fresh talent you'll have for your Star Dazzle show!"

Sharpay forgot her vow to show good yoga-class manners. "Mother, did you *hear* what I just *said*?" she yelled. Frustrated, she turned to her brother. "Ryan, talk to Mother."

Ryan obediently twisted himself into a new position to smile at his mother. "Hi, Mum."

She beamed back at him. "Ducky! How's my dashing boy?" She nodded towards Sharpay. "Tell pumpkin if she worries too much, she'll get frown lines."

Sharpay stormed out of the class. If her mother wouldn't fix this situation, she'd deal with it herself!

Mr Fulton was walking down the hall by the spa when he was suddenly pulled aside by a very angry Sharpay.

"I want them out!" she ordered.

Mr Fulton sighed. "Your mother specifically said–"

"Don't mention that backstabbing yogini to me!" Sharpay said. She paused to think for a moment, then suggested, "If you can't fire them, make them want to quit."

He suppressed a groan. "Actually," he explained, "we do need the help."

Sharpay could tell she wasn't going to get her way this time . . . at least not completely. But she could still win the war, even if she didn't win the battle. "Well, if they think working here is going to be summer camp," she said in a steely voice, "they're in for a surprise."

Lava Springs' newest employees were standing around the kitchen, waiting to start their jobs. They looked at their geeky uniforms and tried to remember why they all wanted summer jobs. Oh, yeah . . . to put some money in the bank.

There was one particular Wildcat, however, who would have been happy to be there even if he didn't earn a pay cheque.

"Chef Michael is going to teach me the art of Austrian flake pastry, and Sharpay's going to be where I work," Zeke said with excitement. "How much better can summer get?"

Chad rolled his eyes. "A real dream come true."

Zeke looked at him earnestly. "If you actually get to know her, she's—"

Chad shuddered. "Dude, be my guest."

"Hey, I had no idea about Sharpay," Troy said quickly. "Mr Fulton just said there were Wildcats fans at Lava Springs and jobs were available. So let's go for it."

Suddenly, Mr Fulton appeared from nowhere. He looked at them sternly. "Indeed, since your jobs will be fleeting if you continue to treat your employment as if it's recess."

Chad was insulted. "Recess? Sir, we're actually in high school."

Mr Fulton sneered. "As evidenced by the little toy you seem to carry at all times?"

Puzzled, Chad glanced down at his hands. Oh.

"It's a basketball, sir," he explained.

"Better known at Lava Springs as a non-approved recreation device," Mr Fulton said as he took the basketball from Chad. He tossed uniforms at the Wildcats and snapped out their assignments. "Danforth and Bolton, waiters and, when needed, caddies. Jason, dishwasher. Miss McKessie, I'm told you're efficient . . ."

She beamed as he handed her a clipboard.

"You'll handle member activities. Keep me in sight at all times. Kelsi, piano at lunchtime and cocktail hour. That means mood music, not new music. Clear? Martha, chopping, cutting and preparing plates. Please complete the summer with the equal number of digits that I assume you currently possess. Zeke, you'll assist Chef Michael in . . ."

As the chef pulled trays of fresh scones from the oven, Zeke said happily, "The promised land."

At that moment, Gabriella rushed into the kitchen. Mr Fulton looked at his watch and raised one eyebrow.

"Um, Mr Fulton, Your Excellency, sir, is it okay if we draw straws to see who has to wait on Sharpay?" Chad asked in an innocent voice.

"Henceforth, none of you will be *waiting* on *Sharpay*," Mr Fulton said.

"Snap!" Chad grinned.

Mr Fulton continued frostily, "You'll be *serving Miss Evans*."

Jason looked confused. "What's that?"

Mr Fulton sighed. He'd spent so many summers training high-school students, and he had so many more summers to go before he could retire ... sometimes the thought made him weary.

"Always address our members as Mr, Mrs or Miss. Let's practise," he suggested. He faced Jason and pretended to be waiting on him. "Miss Evans, would you care for lemonade?"

"Actually, I'm not Miss Evans," Jason said, feeling even more confused. "I'm Jason."

Taylor whispered to Gabriella. "This is going to be a long summer."

Mr Fulton looked at Chad. "Mr Danforth, summon your 'high school' expertise to demonstrate member protocol for us. Miss—"

Chad gritted his teeth and said, "... *Evans* ... more lemonade ... your royal blondeness?"

Mr Fulton decided that that would have to do. He faced his new summer employees and said, "Do clock in on time. Three infractions of any kind and your employment is terminated." He glanced at Gabriella and looked at his watch again. "It would seem your break ended a minute and a half ago, Miss Montez. Let's hope no members drowned in your absence."

He turned on his heel and exited the kitchen as swiftly as possible.

"Okay . . . that man officially scares me," Martha said.

Chad nodded. "Suddenly I'm missing Ms Darbus," he admitted. "How sick is that?"

Troy decided it was time to get everyone focusing on the positive. "Guys, there's a hoop out back, we get two free meals a day, and we only wear geeky outfits when on duty. All for one, one for all. Come on now, it's our summer."

They all brightened up.

"What team?" Chad yelled.

"Wildcats!" they all yelled back.

After a second, Jason asked the question he'd been puzzling over for some time. "Does anyone know what 'henceforth' means?"

CHAPTER FOUR

Sharpay's fellow Wildcats did have a lot of work to do, and Mr Fulton did not make it easy for them. They had to clean off dining tables as soon as a meal was finished. They had to cart dirty dishes to the kitchen. They had to push the drinks trolley around the club. They had to pick up used towels, arrange rolls in breadbaskets and generally help out whenever they were needed, quickly and with a smile.

Mr Fulton watched them closely, correcting them any time they made a mistake.

If Chad was too slow cleaning off the dining tables, Mr Fulton told him to speed it up.

And when Gabriella missed a towel that had been left under a bush by the pool? Mr Fulton told her to 'secure the perimeter' by looking everywhere for lost flip-flops, used towels and misplaced water bottles.

But when Mr Fulton's back was turned, the Wildcats knew how to have fun.

If Troy had to take dirty glasses to the kitchen, he took a spin on the cart after he'd emptied it!

If Chad had to fill a dozen breadbaskets, he threw the dinner rolls across the kitchen with a pair of tongs.

It was fun, but it was also tiring. At the end of another long day of work, Gabriella plodded into the staff room carrying an armload of used towels. She dumped them in a laundry basket, and slid her time card into the clock to punch out.

A hand reached over her shoulder holding another time card. She turned to see Troy looking down at her.

"Ever been on a golf course?" he asked.

"We're employees, Troy, not members," she reminded him. "And I don't play golf."

He raised his eyebrows. "Who said anything about playing golf?"

When they got out to the golf course, Gabriella saw that Troy had set up a picnic under large, shady trees on the green.

She looked around nervously. "You sure it's okay to be out here?"

"Unless the jackrabbits turn us in," he said with a grin.

Gabriella laughed, feeling relaxed and happy for the first time all day.

But at that very moment, Sharpay and Ryan were standing on the roof of the country club. Sharpay whipped open a shoulder bag that had slots for binoculars, walkie-talkies and a digital camera. She frowned at Troy and Gabriella through the binoculars.

"I have no idea what anyone sees in her," she

said through gritted teeth.

"Hard to figure," Ryan agreed. "Since coming to East High she's starred in the winter musical, won the Academic Decathlon, made friends with everyone on campus and is dating the most popular boy in Albuquerque."

Sharpay tossed her head in disgust. "She's wearing last year's colours."

"And picnicking is a non-approved golf-course activity," Ryan added.

But Sharpay wasn't listening. "I am an outstanding student – if you overlook maths, science, social studies and history. I'm a five-time Star Dazzle winner, have won three 'most innovative hairdo' badges from Girl Scouts and am *massively* fashion forward. I've been at East High three years, and she's been there five minutes. Isn't it obvious that Troy Bolton deserves to be with me?" She handed him the binoculars.

"Somehow that doesn't seem like his immediate plan," Ryan observed.

"His plan's about to change," Sharpay snapped.

Out on the golf course, Gabriella was unaware that she and Troy were being watched. Instead, she was enjoying a perfect summer evening with Troy.

"So how's kitchen duty?" she asked.

"The team that washes dishes together, wins together," Troy said.

Gabriella nodded. "My mum said summer jobs look good on college applications."

"All part of that frightening concept called 'the future'," Troy said glumly.

She gave him a searching look. "You sound a little worried."

"Hey, college costs a fortune," Troy said. "My parents are saving pennies. Unlike the people at this place."

"You're a cinch for a scholarship," she said.

He shrugged. "I can't rely on that. I'm only as good as whatever happens next season."

"Let's decide that the future doesn't start until September," Gabriella said. "I've never been in one place for an entire summer, Troy, and certainly never with–"

She stopped, suddenly feeling shy.

". . . a supremely gifted sandwich maker like me?" Troy said, rescuing her.

She smiled. "I want to remember this summer," she answered softly.

He jumped up, pulled her to her feet, and began dancing with her in the warm light of the setting sun. Gabriella laughed as he dipped her, then pulled her up and twirled her around.

And, for the moment, the glow of the present made them forget all about the future.

That glow wouldn't last, of course. Not if Sharpay had anything to say about it

Mr Hardy, one of the club's maintenance workers, had just put his feet up when his walkie-talkie squawked.

Sighing, he picked it up.

"Mr Hardy, Sharpay Evans here," she said crisply. "When I was on the fourth fairway today, it seemed . . . bone dry. Could you give it a little extra splash?"

"Right away, Miss Evans," he said, happy that he wasn't being asked to do something major. He hit a few buttons and sat down again, ready to get back to some peace and quiet.

Troy and Gabriella's dance had just come to an end. They stood facing each other, leaning towards each other, on the verge of a kiss . . . when a dozen high-powered sprinklers came on, completely drenching them!

They laughed as they started running. They were having as much fun as they did when they ran through lawn sprinklers as little kids.

Sharpay scowled as she saw that her prank had failed.

"That sort of looks like fun," Ryan said wistfully.

Sharpay lowered her binoculars. "Does it?" she said slowly as an idea formed in her mind.

She picked up her phone and punched in a number.

Seconds later, Mr Fulton's phone rang. When

he saw who was calling, he winced, but he did what he had to do. He answered it.

"This is a private club, not a water park," Mr Fulton lectured Troy and Gabriella, who were standing in front of him, dripping wet. "We exist to serve our membership. Employees will do well to remember their place. Clear?"

Troy and Gabriella nodded meekly.

Mr Fulton turned his laser eyes on Gabriella. "Late back from your break today, now frolicking on the golf course. We're not off to an auspicious start, Miss Montez."

Sharpay watched the lecture through her binoculars and said to Ryan, "Keep an eye on them tomorrow and keep me posted."

"Why are you smiling?" Ryan asked warily. "You're scaring me now."

Sharpay just smiled. "There's nothing to worry about, Ryan. This is *our* campus, remember?"

CHAPTER FIVE

Early the next morning, Kelsi went to the country club's dining room and began to play a song she had composed.

In the staff room, Troy and Gabriella heard the music as they clocked in. They glanced at each other and headed to the lounge. Ryan entered the room, but when he saw who was there, he hid behind a potted plant. As he listened to Kelsi play, he began to look concerned. This song was excellent.

"Whoa, sounding good, Wildcat!" Gabriella said.

Kelsi immediately stopped playing and covered the music. "Actually, I have to get ready for the ladies' bridge luncheon. I won't exactly be rocking out." She glanced over at her friends and added excitedly, "But we'll all really have fun in the club's talent show, because employees do a number and I've got ideas for everyone . . . You guys sing lead, and Zeke and Chad and everyone can do backup and maybe dance, too, and . . ."

Behind the potted palm, Ryan whispered into his walkie-talkie, "Goldenthroat, this is Hatboy. We may have trouble."

Sharpay and her mother were in the spa, their faces slathered with avocado. As Sharpay listened to her brother's walkie-talkie, she raised one eyebrow. Very interesting . . .

Back in the dining room, Troy held up his hands to stop Kelsi. "Club talent show? Whoa, whoa!" he said. "Big time-out on that one. My singing career began and ended with the East High

Winter Musical. I'm only here to make a cheque and sneak into the pool after work."

Kelsi's face fell. "Oh."

Ryan smiled. Sharpay will be relieved to hear this, he thought as he left the dining room.

Troy looked at Gabriella. She'd back him up on this, right?

Gabriella asked Kelsi, "What was that piece you were playing a minute ago?"

"Oh . . . nothing." Kelsi shrugged. "It's really just . . . nothing."

Gabriella picked up the sheet music and turned it over. At the top of the page, were the words "Troy and Gabriella's Song." Eyebrows raised, she said, "What's this about?"

Kelsi looked sheepish. "I was thinking if you guys did a show next year at school . . . you know . . . I wanted to be ready."

Once Ryan was outside by the pool, he called his sister again on his walkie-talkie. "You want the bad news or the good news?" he asked.

"Just spill it, Ryan!" Sharpay snapped as beautician put cucumber slices on her eyes. She took a sip from her smoothie. "I'm busy!"

"I heard Kelsi working on an amazing new song, and she didn't write it for us," he whispered. "But the good news is that Troy announced that he doesn't want anything to do with our Star Dazzle show."

Gabriella glanced over at Troy as she said to Kelsi, "Well, can we at least hear the song you're working on? It does have our name on it . . . ." Kelsi hesitated, so Gabriella reached over and played the first few notes. That was enough. Kelsi sat down and began to play.

After a few moments, Kelsi was playing with such total concentration that she didn't even notice when the other Wildcats poked their heads in from the kitchen to listen.

When she finished playing, however, she did hear something: wild applause as her friends burst into the dining room.

"Wow, I love that song," Gabriella said.

"I've got the talent show sign-up sheet right here," Taylor said. "The kitchen staff said it's really fun. How about it?"

Everyone nodded in agreement, but they looked at Troy. What would he say?

"Well, I guess we could croak something out if we had to," he said. "But it's got to be all of us."

Kelsi signed Taylor's sheet as the other Wildcats all gave each other high fives.

Sharpay took a sip of her smoothie. "I've been thinking, Ryan, it might actually be a wonderful idea if Troy participates in our show."

Ryan frowned. "But if he sings with Gabriella, our talent show is going to be . . ."

"Oh, I'm not certain Gabriella is ideally suited to help Troy realize his full potential here at Lava Springs," she said airily. She turned to her mother. "Mummy, what time is Daddy going to be here?"

"We tee off at noon," her mother replied. "Join us?"

"Wonderful," Sharpay said. She pulled a cucumber off her face and ate it with a loud snap.

Later that day, the Wildcats were busy in the kitchen. Martha was chopping vegetables, Zeke was baking, Jason was washing dishes and Troy and Chad were putting food on a serving trolley. Only Kelsi had some time off, so she was thumbing through music at one of the prep tables.

Suddenly Mr Fulton appeared carrying two white overalls. He tossed them to Troy and Chad, barking, "Danforth, Bolton, you're caddying today: 40 bucks a bag. You've been requested."

"By who?" Troy asked.

"Who cares?" Chad said, delighted. "For 40 bucks I'd caddy for Godzilla."

"That's the spirit," Mr Fulton said.

Troy and Chad walked to the first tee and saw Sharpay and Ryan waiting.

"Hi, boys!" Sharpay said happily. "So, Troy, I thought it was time for you to meet my parents."

Troy shuddered. 'Meeting the parents'

sounded like something a boyfriend would do. Still, he smiled politely and shook hands with Sharpay's mother.

He looked around. "So . . . where's your dad?"

As if on cue, a stretch limo rolled into the parking lot. A man wearing expensive golf clothes stepped out and strode over to them.

"Where's the first tee and what's the course record?" he called out. He saw the boys gaping at him and chuckled. "Just kidding . . . I built the course myself and hold the record. But who's counting?"

He gave Sharpay a big hug and slapped Ryan on the back. Then he turned to Troy and Chad. "So . . . quite a season you boys had."

"Troy played for the golf team, too, Daddy," Sharpay said sweetly.

Her father looked impressed. "Versatile." He asked Chad, "What about you, son?"

"Track and field," Chad said.

Mrs Evans laughed. "Might come in handy today, with the way I play golf. Fair warning."

Sharpay beamed as she handed Troy her father's golf bag. This meeting couldn't be going any better if she had scripted it herself – which, in a way, she had.

Her mother teed off, sending her ball off into the rocks that edged the course. Then her father hit his first shot. The golf ball sailed into the air. The game had started.

Sharpay got into her cart and rolled across the green. She had her very own golf cart, of course. It was pink and included a DVD player, an ice chest and a smoothie maker.

Soon Mr Evans was asking Troy's advice before every shot. At the ninth hole, Troy sized up the lay of the land, then said, "One forty-three to the pin, downhill lie, elevated green. I'd go with the seven iron, sir."

Mr Evans swung his golf club. He watched as the ball sailed through the air and landed right next to the flag! "Nice call, son," he said.

Sharpay applauded. Troy smiled modestly and then looked around for Chad, who was knee-deep in brambles, looking for a ball that Ryan had sliced into the woods. As a branch nearly hit him in the face, he resolved that he would never complain about washing dishes again.

At that moment, Sharpay hit her golf ball. Chad and Troy both had to dive to the ground to avoid being hit in the head.

"Why don't you take up knitting, Sharpay?" Chad suggested. "That way you can only injure yourself."

As the day went on, Troy was surprised to find that he was actually having fun. It was sunny, and he enjoyed helping Mr Evans play a good game. If Sharpay and her ridiculous pink cart hadn't been there, he wouldn't have had a care in the world.

As he and Mr Evans walked past the clubhouse on their way to the next hole, he looked over the fence surrounding the pool. He saw Gabriella sitting on her lifeguard stand and said, "Dinner tonight? Then sneak a swim?"

She nodded happily, but as she watched him

rejoin the Evans family, her smile dimmed. Sharpay handed Troy a cold drink. Even from a distance, Gabriella could tell she was flirting with him – and Troy was smiling!

He has to be nice to her, Gabriella thought, trying to be fair. That's his job.

But still, she felt her heart sink a little as she watched them walk across the grass.

After the golf party had played several more holes, Sharpay suggested, "Daddy, why not let Troy try a shot?"

Mr Evans was so impressed with Troy's golf tips that he agreed without hesitation.

Troy smacked the ball onto the green, and the Evanses all applauded. In that moment, Troy felt a change. He wasn't a caddy working for the Evans family any more. Now he was another golfer playing with them.

Sharpay floored her golf cart to pick up Troy.

Chad had to dive for the ground, this time to avoid being run over. "I'm saving up for a car, saving up for a car," he murmured to himself.

Troy hit another great shot, and the Evans family oohed and aahed.

"Tiger Woods would have been proud to hit that shot!" Mrs Evans exclaimed.

"Absolutely," Sharpay said, adding casually, "and what a shame that a potential all-star for the University of Albuquerque Redhawks is clearing away dirty dishes."

Her father took the bait. "They've got Troy working in the kitchen?" he asked, shocked.

Troy hit another shot. The white ball flew into the sky in a long, graceful arc.

Mr Evans watched the perfect shot and said, "I've seen Troy play basketball. And I'm sure the Redhawks will be interested in his future."

Chad shot a suspicious look at Sharpay. What was she up to? he thought.

"That's inspired, Daddy," she said warmly. "Troy is very concerned about college."

Her father smiled at her, pleased. She smiled back, even more pleased. Everything was going according to plan.

CHAPTER SIX

Later, Chad sat in the kitchen, his sore feet immersed in an ice-filled bucket.

"Next time I see country club princess, I'm gonna launch her and her pink cart straight into the pool," Chad promised.

Mr Fulton came into the kitchen and frowned at him. "Mr Danforth, this is a kitchen, not a nail salon. You and Jason suit up for lunch duty in the dining room." He handed Troy a blue blazer and tie. "Bolton, you've got five minutes to change and come with me."

Surprised, Troy followed Mr Fulton out the door.

"What's with the tie and coat?" Taylor asked.

"Maybe it's a country club version of detention," Jason suggested.

The others looked worried. They didn't know why Troy was being asked to dress so formally – but they knew it probably meant trouble.

Mr Fulton led Troy, now nicely turned out in coat and tie, into the dining room where Sharpay and her father were sitting with some other club members. Chad and Jason began pouring iced tea for the table as Mr Evans said, "Let's talk about your future, Troy."

Troy looked at him, confused. "My . . . future?"

"Daddy's on the board of directors at the University of Albuquerque," Sharpay explained.

"Yep, we've got plenty to talk about," Mr Evans said. "But first . . ." He turned to Jason and Chad. ". . . bring on the food!"

* * *

Yes, the Wildcats were happy to have jobs.

Yes, they all needed to save money for college.

And yes, they all should have been working at that very minute.

But they were concerned about Troy. As Chad and Jason pushed food trolleys out to Troy's table, the others peered from the kitchen door into the dining room.

"What are they doing to him?" Martha asked in a hushed voice.

Zeke shrugged. "Who knows, but that pancetta-wrapped foie gras with seared bay scallops looks amazing," he offered.

"Look, Troy's trying to figure out which fork to use," Kelsi said.

As if she had heard this, Sharpay speared a melon ball with her own fork and fed it to Troy.

"Problem solved," Taylor said dryly.

While Chad and Jason served the food, they heard a member say to Troy, "I saw your championship game. Wow, that shot at the buzzer—"

Troy caught Chad's eye. Quickly, he said, "My team-mates stole the ball, or I wouldn't even have had the chance to—"

"Oh, Troy, you're much too modest," Sharpay broke in. "You were voted MVP for the entire season." She leaned over and retied his tie, saying, "This shirt positively screams for a Windsor knot."

"A what?" Troy couldn't believe it! She was dressing him in front of all these people! He had never felt so mortified in his life!

Gabriella joined her friends at the doorway.

"What's she doing?" Gabriella asked.

"Fixing his tie," Kelsi guessed.

"Or strangling him," Taylor added grimly.

"What are they all talking about?" Gabriella wondered just as Chad passed by with yet another serving tray.

"How Troy single-handedly saved the planet," he said sarcastically.

Just then they heard a foot tapping behind them, and they turned to see . . . Mr Fulton! Quickly, they scattered back to their jobs. Fortunately, Kelsi had to return to the piano and could watch what happened next.

"We've got a heck of a basketball programme at U of A," Mr Evans was saying. "And an excellent scholarship programme."

That got Troy's attention. "Scholarship?"

"Between the bunch of us here, we pull a little weight at the school," Mr. Evans continued. "And it's never too soon to be thinking about your future, son."

Troy suddenly remembered that he'd promised to meet Gabriella. "Oh, man, I'm supposed to clock out. Mr Fulton will—"

"Nonsense!" Mr Evans cried. "You haven't had dessert, and we haven't talked golf."

"Basketball and golf are just the beginning with Troy, Daddy," Sharpay volunteered. "Have you heard him sing?"

What?! Troy quickly said, "Singing? No, no—"

One of the men at the table chuckled. "A singing point guard? Now this I gotta hear."

"Maybe at our Star Dazzle Talent Show," Sharpay said. "Oh, give them a sample, Troy." She turned to cue Kelsi.

"My voice is a little hoarse today," Troy croaked as convincingly as he could. "But thank you so much for the golf and food. It's all been . . . great."

"So . . . you will sing some other time, though, right?" Sharpay asked.

"Promise," he finally said, feeling trapped.

"Perfect!" Sharpay exclaimed. "Dessert?" She signalled for Chad and Jason to bring the dessert trolley. Éclair or tiramisu? Or maybe as a celebration, she'd have both!

By the time Troy had finished his dinner, all of his friends had gone for the night.

He headed outside to the pool, where he found Gabriella cleaning up.

"Sorry I'm late!" he called across the pool.

"Just give me a few more minutes!"

She nodded and called back, "Nice tie. Shoes don't match, though."

He rolled his eyes at the teasing and ran back inside to clock out. Just as he was putting his time card into the machine, Mr Fulton appeared.

"Don't clock out, Bolton," he said.

"But I'm done for the day, sir," Troy replied.

"Evidently not," the manager said. "Your presence is required in the ballroom."

Troy thought of Gabriella, waiting for him – but then he looked at Mr Fulton's face, which had a don't-even-think-about-arguing expression on it. He sighed and followed the manager to the ballroom, where there was a sign that read: CLOSED REHEARSAL/NO ADMITTANCE.

Holding a torch, Mr Fulton led Troy to a chair in the darkened room.

"What the heck . . . ?" Troy started to say.

But Mr Fulton had gone.

Suddenly, the darkness was broken by a brilliant spotlight, which was shining on – of course – Sharpay. She was standing centre stage wearing a Hawaiian princess costume, complete with a pineapple on her head. She was joined by Ryan, Jackie, Lea and Emma, doing a Hawaiian tiki number that involved a chorus of 'humu humu' and 'waka waka'.

Troy stared at the stage, his mouth hanging open. Sharpay was singing and dancing her heart out, and Ryan was reaching for the rafters with every note.

Troy was afraid to move. He felt as if he'd been trapped inside a mega-musical machine.

Out by the pool, Taylor was giving her girl Gabriella some no-nonsense advice. "Honey, ten minutes is being late . . . but an hour is approaching a felony."

"We just talked about having dinner," Gabriella said. "No big deal."

"Just because Troy is a nice guy doesn't mean he's immune to boy disease," Taylor said.

Gabriella raised one eyebrow. "Boy disease?"

Taylor gave her a meaningful look. "Forgetting things he shouldn't forget."

Gabriella laughed. "So now you're a boy expert?"

"My older sister has ten rules about boy behaviour, and nine involve boys forgetting things they shouldn't forget," Taylor said. She added pointedly, "Like dinner dates."

"It wasn't an official date type of thing," Gabriella said, trying to be fair.

Taylor shook her head. "Rule three: all dates are official, whether the boy knows it or not." She paused, then said, "Chad and I are going for pizza with Zeke and Jason. I think Martha and Kelsi are going to meet us. So let's go—"

Gabriella hesitated.

"I'll meet you there," she finally said. "Troy will probably want to come, too."

Taylor sighed. She certainly hoped Troy's case of boy disease didn't get any worse!

CHAPTER SEVEN

When the Hawaiian tiki number was finally, mercifully, over, Troy applauded politely.

Sharpay jumped down off the stage, beaming at him. "So?" she asked. "You love it?"

Troy hesitated, eyeballing the pineapple on her head. "Look, do you ever just . . . sing? Without lights, sets and all the backup people?"

Sharpay gave him a puzzled look. "It would be much harder to get applause that way."

"I'm not talking about applause . . . or volcanoes," Troy said. "I'm talking about hanging with friends. Doing nothing. Singing for fun."

Sharpay considered this. "Wait a minute, not doing anything . . . that might work." She paused. "A dark stage," she said dramatically. "A single spotlight. We break out of darkness into the circle of light . . ."

"We?" Troy asked uneasily.

But Sharpay didn't seem to hear him. "No set, no frills. Just you and me," she went on. "Simple, dramatic. That's a wonderful idea, Troy! We could do it in our club talent show."

When Ryan overheard that, a tiny frown wrinkled his forehead. What was Sharpay talking about? *He* was singing with her in the club talent show . . .

Troy looked horrified. "I'm here to work," he said. "Saving money for my . . . future. Being onstage is really your thing, not mine."

She smiled at him sweetly. "It could be . . . *our* thing," Sharpay said coyly.

"What?! Whoa. I've already got an 'our thing' with Gabriella, which I'm very late for at the moment."

"But the show could be so . . ." Her voice trailed off, but she was still gazing at him.

Troy had to get out of there – now! Trying to distract Sharpay, he blurted out, "Hey, those are *really* nice shoes you're wearing."

Sharpay glanced down. "You like them? I bought them in New York. I have them in nine colours."

And when she looked up, Troy had gone.

Gabriella had finally finished picking up all the wet towels when she heard someone behind her yell, "CANNONBALL!"

Troy came running across the deck and jumped into the pool, fully dressed.

"Whoa, you're crazy, Wildcat!" She laughed.

"And *so* late," he admitted. "But I have food. A candle for a poolside picnic. And Zeke made desserts." He grinned. "But first, I dare you . . ."

She grinned back. "I've got to go put my suit on," she began.

"What happened to Miss Fun Kindergarten?" Troy said.

"CANNONBALL!" she yelled as she leaped into the water.

They both started laughing hysterically and splashing each other.

"Hey, you have no idea what I just saw," Troy said. "I'll never be able to look at a pineapple again."

"Huh?"

He laughed. "Never mind. You know, right now with you, it's finally feeling like summer."

"Yeah." Gabriella smiled. "It is."

They moved a little closer to each other in the moonlight, romance fairly shimmering in the air, but just as they were about to kiss—

"Well, well," Mr Fulton said. "The water bugs are back."

Troy and Gabriella, startled, whirled around as Mr Fulton turned on a torch and levelled its beam at them. They climbed out of the pool.

Troy gulped. "It was my idea, Mr Fulton, she didn't . . ."

The manager shook his head sternly. "You have a reason to be here after-hours, Mr Bolton.

Miss Montez, however, does not." He frowned at Gabriella. "I overlooked the tardiness yesterday. But then came the golf-course jaunt, and now this. Two days, two strikes. Don't get a third."

He walked back into the clubhouse. Just inside the door, Sharpay smiled – she'd seen the whole thing.

Later that evening, Troy took his basketball out to the driveway to shoot some hoops with his dad. After a few minutes, he said to his father, "Sharpay's dad let me play a few holes today. Then he introduced me to some U of A graduates in the dining room."

His dad stopped guarding him for a second. "What graduates?"

Troy took advantage of the opportunity to sink a basket. "Mr Sherwood, Mr Langdon. They're members at Lava Springs."

"I played ball with those guys," his dad said, pleased. "I'll give them a call. This is great news."

"Really?"

His dad nodded. "Shaking hands with influential people doesn't hurt."

"But they were talking about scholarships right in front of Jason and Chad, who were like . . . serving food to me," Troy said.

"And getting paid for it," his dad pointed out. "It's called a job. You were invited, nothing wrong with that."

Troy shrugged. "It felt weird."

"I love that you've got the team working together at the club," his dad said. "But senior year is coming up, Troy. You're not going to be a Wildcat forever. Team is about now, but everyone has their own future."

"I'm not sure what you mean." Troy was confused. Wasn't his dad always saying that to be a team leader he had to remember the team?

His dad sighed. "As life goes on, lots of dogs are chasing the same bones. But one dog gets there first. You've earned your opportunities, son. A scholarship is special because they don't give it to everyone—"

Troy nodded. He wasn't happy about it, but he knew what his dad was saying was right. "I get it, Dad."

"Okay." Mr Bolton nodded, then decided to lighten the mood. "So . . . how was the food?"

Troy smiled. "Insanely good," he admitted.

The next morning, Troy raced over to the pool before starting work, hoping to find Gabriella so he could apologize. She was in her lifeguard chair as Taylor led a water-aerobics class.

"Still haven't gotten all the water out of my ears," he said to Gabriella. "Didn't mean to get you in trouble."

"And vice versa," she said.

He smiled. "So maybe today we can—"

But he was interrupted by a muffled voice saying, "Oh, Troy?"

His smile faded as he turned to see Sharpay inside the clubhouse, knocking on the window to get his attention. She held up a handwritten sign that read: MR FULTON'S OFFICE.

He turned back to Gabriella. "Anyway, what time is your lunch break?"

"Troy!" Sharpay cried, pointing insistently at her sign.

"One-thirty," Gabriella replied.

"The free cheeseburgers are on me," he said. "See you then?"

She nodded happily, and he went inside.

Taylor climbed out of the pool. "What's that girl up to?" she asked, as Sharpay followed Troy.

"Who knows?" Gabriella shrugged.

"Believe me," Taylor said darkly, "she does."

When Troy got to the kitchen to clock in, Kelsi was already there talking excitedly about the talent show. As Troy walked past them, the other Wildcats started saying something. It sounded liked "humu, humu!"

Troy stopped. He turned and stared at them.

They looked back innocently.

But as he walked on, they started again. This time, they were saying "waka, waka!"

Shaking his head, he grabbed his waiter's jacket. As he was buttoning it, Mr Fulton appeared.

Quickly, Troy said, "I'm sorry I'm a couple of minutes late, Mr Fulton. And the pool thing last night, you can't blame Gabriella, she only–"

"I'm promoting you," Mr Fulton interrupted.

Troy couldn't believe it. "You are?"

The other Wildcats were close enough to overhear this. They all exchanged surprised glances.

The manager cracked a tiny smile. "There's an opening as an assistant to the golf pros. Salaried job, no clocking in. You start immediately."

"But . . ." Troy was too stunned to finish.

"Five hundred dollars per week," the manager said.

"WHAT!!! Per week?! Oh, man, that's totally off the hook!" Troy managed to collect himself. "I mean . . . that sounds very . . . workable."

Mr Fulton led Troy out of the kitchen, telling him his new duties as they walked. They ended up at a door with a sign that read: MEN'S LOCKER

Room – Members Only. Inside, Troy got to see how the members lived. The locker room was nice. Really nice.

But he was too distracted to notice much. He asked Mr Fulton, "I'll be teaching golf?"

"To kids," the manager said, rolling his eyes a bit. "Oh, the joy."

"I don't think I'm qualified," he protested.

Mr Fulton sighed. "Show the little angels which end of the club to hold, tee up a ball, then duck. There's more. The board is extending membership privileges to you for the summer. You have full use of club facilities. So be prudent, and . . ." He pointed to a locker with Troy's name on it. ". . . congratulations."

"Whoa," Troy said.

Mr Fulton snapped his fingers and a locker-room attendant appeared holding a rack of fashionable new golf clothes for Troy.

Troy's mind was reeling. This was all happening so fast! Then he opened his locker and found a golf bag with new clubs. His name was

71

emblazoned on the bag. He pulled out a five iron, took a couple of practise swings, and broke out into a huge grin.

"Save it for the first tee," Mr Fulton said. "And to get there, this might come in handy."

He handed Troy a key. "That's for your golf cart. It's number 14. Same as your basketball uniform, I'm told. Questions?"

Troy looked from the clothes to the locker to the golf clubs to the key. "How did this happen?"

Mr Fulton raised one eyebrow. "Evidently, Sharpay Evans feels you have untapped potential." He lowered his voice to offer a little advice. "Young man, the future is a big place, and the Evans family has real clout. I suggest you take the ride."

Troy was still amazed, but he nodded slowly. Maybe Mr Fulton was right . . .

CHAPTER EIGHT

O ver at the pool, Gabriella was busy scrubbing tiles. She didn't mind working hard, but she couldn't help but feel a little resentful when Sharpay walked by looking amazing.

The other club girls and Ryan were lounging by the pool, working on their tans.

Sharpay struck a pose to show off her outfit. "Is the green piping too much?"

Just as she expected, Emma immediately said, "Green is *so* this year," and the other club girls nodded in agreement. Each of them wore a swimsuit in a different shade of green.

Sharpay spoke a little louder so that Gabriella would hear. "I'm taking a golf lesson from Troy Bolton, so I want to look just right."

Sharpay's friends sighed in unison. Troy Bolton! He was such a cutie!

As Sharpay left, she said to Gabriella, "The pool has never looked better! Brava!"

Gabriella just gritted her teeth and scrubbed harder. Ryan watched them from the other side of the pool. His sister had always acted this way, but, for some reason, today it was making him rather uncomfortable.

Over at the junior golf clinic, Troy ducked as a club whistled past his head. He tried to figure out how to get the kids to focus on the finer points of the game.

"Bolton, your 11:30 is here," one of the other golf pros called.

Troy looked up to see Sharpay waving at him. He looked back at the members of his junior golf clinic. All of a sudden, spending the morning with them didn't seem so bad.

Ryan glanced over at Gabriella. She was still scrubbing tiles. And it was so hot out . . .

Before he knew it, he walked over to her. "If you ever decide to dump my sister into the pool, give me a warning so that I can be here."

Gabriella could hear the sympathy in his voice. She said, "Does she ever actually swim, or does she just *look* at the pool all summer?"

Ryan laughed. "Sharpay doesn't allow her hair near water without shampoo, conditioner and blow dryer within reach." He hesitated, then added shyly, "Look . . . um . . . I just want to say that I think it's cool that you're here. Last year's lifeguard was fat and had a hairy back."

Oops. That hadn't come out quite right.

But Gabriella just said, in a teasing voice, "I guess that's a compliment."

"Oh, absolutely," he said, fumbling to say something that sounded cool. "I mean, entirely."

She decided to help him out. "It was fun watching you dance in the spring show, Ryan. Especially when Sharpay wasn't dancing in front of you. You were amazing."

"*Really*?" Ryan's heart skipped a beat.

"Like, big-time." She smiled. "I'm looking forward to seeing you in the club talent show."

There was a brief silence. "Okay, well . . . thanks again," he said. "I mean, not for what you just said about my dancing, but for just being here. By the pool. On a nice day and everything. I guess they pay you to do that, right?" He stopped. He had *totally* lost where he was going with this! "I guess I'll swim now. I'm not that good a swimmer, but . . . lifeguard on duty . . ."

As he walked to the edge of the pool, Gabriella said, "Ryan? You want to put on a swimsuit."

He looked down. Oh. Right. He was still wearing his street clothes.

"Point taken," he said sheepishly.

* * *

Thwack! Sharpay hit a golf ball with a wild swing as Troy looked on. The ball went flying to the right.

Thwack! This ball veered wildly to the left. *Thwack*! Her next ball headed towards a group of club members, who ducked.

Taylor rounded up the junior golfers for another activity, but she kept a close eye on Sharpay and Troy. She knew that girl was up to something!

Another ball whizzed off in the wrong direction. Troy didn't think he had ever seen a worse golfer.

"By the end of summer you'll have me playing like a pro," Sharpay said cheerfully.

He ducked away from one of her wild swings and muttered, "If I live that long."

She smiled and swung again. "I'm *so* excited about the Star Dazzle Talent Show. We'll find something great to do."

Troy sighed. "I already told you that's not for me."

She ignored him and went on. "Here's the

best news: all the Redhawk coaches and the whole scholarship committee will be there."

Even from a distance, Taylor could see Troy reacting to something Sharpay had said. Reacting with interest and even . . . pleasure. She shook her head in disapproval.

"Really?" Troy said.

"Of course," she said casually, "Daddy and Mummy are on the university booster board. We'll lock up your scholarship with a high C, right from centre stage." She added, "We're all in this together, right?"

Troy shook his head. He had to hold firm. Besides, he'd promised Gabriella and the other guys that he would sing with them. "Your family is being very nice, Sharpay. But singing with you isn't part of my job."

"I know," she said sweetly. "It's just something you promised to do. Remember?" She paused to let him take that in, then said, "You look fabulous in your new clothes, by the way."

He knew she was working him, but it always

felt good to get a compliment. He said, "You like the shoes? They're Italian."

Taylor overheard this comment, and wished she hadn't. She rolled her eyes in despair.

Troy decided it was time to go back to the lesson. He moved forward to show Sharpay the proper – and, he hoped, safer – way to swing her club. He put his arms around her, helping her to adjust her grip. Just then, Gabriella came out of the clubhouse carrying two boxed lunches. Her smile vanished when she saw Troy with his arms around Sharpay.

Taylor met up with Gabriella just as Chad came outside. Taylor nodded towards Sharpay. "That girl has more moves than an octopus in a wrestling match."

"I don't see him running away," Chad said.

"Troy can handle himself," Gabriella said. Now Troy was laughing at something Sharpay said as he moved closer to help her with her swing again. The two of them looked very, very cosy. Gabriella's heart sank a bit.

"Think so?" Taylor said. "He's asking her for her opinion on his new 'Italian' golf shoes."

Gabriella's heart sank a bit more. "He didn't ask me."

"So wake up, sister," Taylor said. "Sharpay is basically offering him a college education just to sing with her in the talent show."

"He'll never do that," Chad protested.

Taylor shook her head. Everywhere she looked, she saw the same thing: denial. "You got eyes?" she said to Chad. "Use 'em."

As Troy helped Sharpay set up another shot, one of the golf pros walked over. "Fulton wants you in the lobby, Troy." Troy nodded and hopped into his golf cart, heading off for the clubhouse.

Once he had gone, Sharpay put a ball on the tee, swung – and smacked it straight down the fairway! She smiled in satisfaction. Of course, she had been taking lessons forever – but Sharpay was nothing if not a great actress.

* * *

When Troy hurried into the lobby, he was surprised to see Mr Fulton and Sharpay's dad – along with three star players from the University of Albuquerque basketball team!

"Troy Bolton, this is–" Mr Evans began.

"I've seen them all play at U of A," Troy interrupted, impressed.

"Come for a practise session up at our gym tonight," one of the players said.

Troy gulped and glanced over at Mr Evans. "Play . . . with you guys?"

The player smiled as if he knew how Troy was feeling. "You're in, bro."

"Wow," Troy said. "That's awesome!"

"Excellent," Mr Evans said. "Now let's all get some awesome lunch."

Troy's head was still spinning when Sharpay scurried up to him and held a tie in front of his face. "I knew it!" she cried. "Coral blue. It's perfect for your skin tones. And mine, too. We're majorly skin-tone compatible, Troy."

"I have no idea what that means," he said, dazed.

"You don't need to," Sharpay said. "I'm here for you." And pretty soon, she thought, you won't know how you got by without me!

A short time later, Troy was hanging out with the Redhawks on the terrace. He couldn't believe it, but they actually wanted his advice – about golf! As they sat down to eat, a cheeseburger was placed in front of him. He was so caught up in the moment that he didn't even look around as he said, "Actually, I think I asked for Swiss on the burger."

Behind him, Chad couldn't believe what he just heard – and he had now officially had enough! He started to pull off his jacket, ready to rumble right there, when someone grabbed his collar and pulled him back.

"Table three needs more iced tea," Mr Fulton said into his ear.

Chad went to the other table, then burst into the kitchen, where Gabriella and Taylor were eating lunch.

"You were right," he said to Taylor. "There's a

guy out there who looks just like Troy, but I don't know who he really is."

Later that day, Ryan and Kelsi were sitting at the piano, when Sharpay swept into the room and headed straight over to them.

Ryan brightened when he saw her. "Hey, Kelsi's got great ideas to spark up the show," he said enthusiastically. "She—"

"I'm thrilled," Sharpay said tersely. She turned to Kelsi and snapped, "That duet you were playing the other morning for Troy and Gabriella, I'm told it's very good. I need it."

Kelsi tried to sound brave. "Actually, that's not available."

Sharpay gave Kelsi a dangerous stare. "Repeat?"

Kelsi felt her firm resolve waver a bit, but she said, "It's something I wrote *for* Troy and Gabriella. In case they—"

"You're an employee here, not a fairy god-mother," Sharpay said. "Transpose the key. Troy and I will be doing it in the talent show. And brighten up the tempo a little bit. We'll need to keep people awake after the other member acts."

She headed for the dining room but Ryan jumped up and grabbed her.

"What about 'Humu Humu'?" he asked.

Sharpay sighed impatiently. "Change in plans."

"What am I supposed to do with my tiki warrior outfit?" Ryan protested.

"Save it for Halloween, go to a luau, sell it on eBay, I don't know," Sharpay snapped. "But in the meantime, keep an eye on those Wildcats. If they're planning on being in the talent show – which I doubt, once they hear about Troy and me – I don't want any surprises." She paused, then added graciously, "And I'll find a song for you somewhere in the show. Or the next show."

"Really? Don't strain yourself, slick," her brother muttered. Then he stalked off.

Sharpay shook her head. "Entertainers are so . . . temperamental."

♩ CHAPTER NINE

Five, four, three, two, one . . . Yes! It was five o'clock and the workday was finally over! Everybody else was getting changed for the staff softball game that evening, so Gabriella wandered outside the kitchen and found Troy there back, shooting hoops.

"Look at you," Gabriella said, taking in the new U of A warm-up jacket he was wearing. "Go team."

"It's a gift from the guys," Troy said, half-sheepish, half-proud.

"The 'guys'?" Gabriella said. "Oh, you mean all those tall people?"

She stole the ball from him and took a shot.

"Right, the Redhawks," Troy said, going for the loose ball. "I've got to go in a minute, but I'll be back in an hour or so. Then can we go to a movie? Promise?"

Gabriella gave him a long, thoughtful look. " 'Promise' is a very big word, Troy."

He hesitated. He knew what she was getting at, but he'd been so busy. "I know . . ."

"And we've got the staff softball game tonight," she reminded him. "Remember, you 'promised' that you'd play?"

"Right . . . softball . . . tonight," he said, trying to cover. "I'll absolutely meet you there."

But he couldn't fool Gabriella. "You forgot, didn't you?"

"No, I just got the days mixed up," he lied. "I'm really sorry about missing lunch today, too. It's been wild. I can't believe how things are working out here."

"Italian golf shoes, new clothes, golf carts," she said coolly. "That's crazy stuff. Hard to keep track of it all, I bet."

"That's just for my job," he said defensively.

"Right . . . the future," she nodded. "That's all I used to worry about, too. Never took my nose out of a book. Then I came to East High, lifted my head up, and liked what I saw." She paused, then added, "It's easy to lose that, I think."

Just then, Chad, Zeke and Jason burst out of the kitchen, ready to play ball.

"Let's see if the Tiger Woods of Toon Town still has a jump shot," Chad said.

That's all it took to get a fast game going among the four of them. Before they had even warmed up, however, they were interrupted by a car pulling up and honking for Troy. The three Redhawk players were there to pick him up.

"Hey, tell them to come over here and mix it up," Zeke said. "We'll give 'em some game."

Troy said awkwardly, "I don't think that's how they roll."

Chad looked at him in disbelief. "That's not how they 'roll'? You think you're on ESPN or something?"

Troy blushed. "We're going to be working out with their coaching staff, I meant."

"Gee, you think maybe you can get us a video?" Chad asked sarcastically.

As Chad stared at Troy, Zeke said, "Yesterday you said we had a two-on-two for after work. Before the softball game."

Chad shook his head. "Zeke, that was so yesterday. You know, when we were all a team."

Troy didn't like leaving everyone angry with him, but the Redhawks were waiting. As he headed towards the car, Chad called out, "Yo, Bolton . . . that's my ball!"

Troy threw him the basketball and got in the car. As the car pulled away, Jason said, "Will you guys be mad if I ask him to get me one of those cool Redhawk jackets?"

Chad and Zeke groaned and shoved Jason who looked, as always, confused.

"What?" he asked.

CHAPTER TEN

On the eighth hole of the golf course, the Wildcats and the rest of the club staff were in the middle of a softball game. A boom box played in the background as team-mates cheered each other on. Life didn't get much better than this!

Back in the car park, Gabriella fired up a golf cart to head over to the game. She spotted Ryan on the way to his car and called out, "Hey, Wildcat, no rehearsal tonight?"

Ryan stopped in his tracks, surprised and a little wary of this friendly greeting. "My sister is working up something new for the talent show," he admitted. "Without me."

"So, you know about the staff softball game tonight?" Gabriella asked.

Ryan felt a faint stirring of hope. Was she actually asking him? No, it wasn't possible. "I'm not staff," he said.

"And I'm not much of a softball player," Gabriella said cheerfully. "So let's go!"

Ryan wasn't sure why she had asked but he didn't care. He hopped in the cart, and they rode off into the warm summer night.

It was the end of an inning. A few Wildcats wandered over to the cart where Gabriella and Ryan were watching the game.

Chad frowned at Ryan. "Did Fulton send you out here to spy on us?"

"Nah," Ryan answered. "My sister did."

"What?" Chad asked.

Everyone looked at him, stunned. Ryan was a little stunned himself – he had always been completely loyal to Sharpay, no matter what. And he was beginning to realize that he'd finally had enough of her. He laughed out loud at how free he suddenly felt. He added, "She thinks you guys might upstage her talent show."

"No worries," Zeke said. "We talked about doing the show, but it looks like Troy has bailed on us. So, whatever."

"What do you mean 'whatever'?" Gabriella asked. "It's our summer, remember. I thought we decided doing the show would be fun?"

Martha raised her hand. "I think so!"

"Who are we kidding?" Chad said. "We don't know what we're doing."

Gabriella pointed at Ryan. "He does."

Everyone looked at Ryan, surprised. He looked back, equally astonished.

"If we had a real director putting it together, we could be great," Gabriella went on. She turned to Ryan. "Have the employees ever won the Star Dazzle award?"

"Hey now," Ryan said, a shock of fear and

excitement running through him at the very thought that Sharpay *might not win*.

"I know what you can do, Ryan," Gabriella said. "So why not do it for us?"

Chad had heard enough. They were athletes, after all, not artists! "Look," he said to Ryan, "if you want to hang, grab a mitt and let's play ball. But we're not dancers, so let's get on with the game."

Ryan heard the dismissive tone in Chad's voice and felt a flare of anger. "You don't think dancing takes some game?" he asked.

He stared right in Chad's eyes.

Chad stared right back.

It was a challenge!

Even as the other Wildcats tried to explain that they didn't dance, and couldn't possibly learn in time for the talent show, Ryan had them doing some baseball moves: throwing, catching, sliding, running bases and swinging the bat. Then he turned each action into a high-energy dance step, and pretty soon the Wildcats were moving and grooving all over the baseball diamond. The improvised dance ended up with Chad sliding into home plate.

Chad got up, dusted himself off and eyed Ryan with new respect. "I'm not saying I'm going to dance in the show, but *if* I did . . . what would we do?"

Everyone turned to look at Ryan. He looked back, feeling both anxious and something else. He noticed they were smiling at him, and he realized what he'd been feeling – a sense of belonging.

Troy was in the middle of the hardest practise session of his life. He was breathing hard as he did his best to outrun, outmanoeuvre and out-jump guys who were bigger, stronger, older . . .

It was work, but it was also really fun.

Troy's dad sat in the stands, watching the practice closely. Sharpay's dad was next to him, keeping his eye on this prospective new recruit that his daughter liked so much. And the University of Albuquerque's Coach Reynolds was under the hoop, noting every move, every step, every block that his players made.

Coach Reynolds blew his whistle for a water break, then walked over to Coach Bolton and Mr Evans. "I like what I'm seeing," he said.

"Troy gives 110, 24-7," his dad said. "That you can count on."

Coach Reynolds nodded thoughtfully. "Have him work on that step-back move. He's got to be able to shoot over the tall dudes."

"Troy hasn't even started growing," Coach Bolton said quickly. "I grew four inches in college. But we'll be working on the step-back, believe me."

Meanwhile Troy wasn't thinking about growing four inches, or working on a step-back move. He was on the sidelines, using his mobile phone.

On the golf course, the softball game had started back up. Gabriella was in the thick of the action, so when her mobile phone rang, she didn't hear it. When Troy's picture came up on the screen, she didn't see it. The phone rang and rang, but was never answered . . .

Later that night, Troy finally drove his dad's truck out to the baseball diamond. The field lights were on, so he hopped out and jogged to the diamond – but it was deserted. All his friends had gone. Troy stood for a long moment at home plate – alone.

Gabriella wrinkled her nose as the smell of chlorine wafted through the morning air. She began getting the pool ready for the day.

Then she looked up to see Ryan strolling towards her. He was wearing a pair of wildly patterned shorts in the Wildcat colours.

"Yo," she said, blinking at the crazy design. "Whoa, Wildcat!"

"Too much?" Ryan asked.

She laughed. "Only in daylight. East High colours, very impressive!"

He relaxed and grinned. "Be true to your school, right?"

"Absolutely," she nodded. Speaking of the Wildcats, that reminded her . . . "And everyone's psyched about the show."

He shrugged, but he looked pleased. "I know they all think I'm Sharpay's poodle, but—"

She held up a hand to stop him before he could become too apologetic. "If they thought that before, they're not thinking it today," she said firmly. He looked unconvinced, so she decided to bolster his confidence. "How do you do that swing-step thing you did last night?"

She awkwardly tried to recreate the move.

Ryan shook his head and said, "More like this . . ."

He demonstrated the move, then he grabbed her hand and spun her around – right into Troy!

Troy, who had decided to stop by to say hello to Gabriella, jumped back in surprise.

"Hey," she said, trying not to look as flustered as she felt.

"Hey," he answered, trying not to raise his eyebrows at the sight of Ryan and Gabriella dancing together.

"Hey," said Ryan, trying to think of something else to say that would ease this awkward moment.

Nope. Nothing came to mind.

Finally, Troy said to Gabriella, "I tried to call. I got . . . hung up at the gym."

"My dad said you did real well with the college guys," Ryan offered.

"They're awesome!" Troy exclaimed. His enthusiasm took over. "Playing with those guys is like another world . . ."

"Go Redhawks," Gabriella said flatly.

Troy's excitement died down. "Really, I tried to call both you and Chad, but . . ."

Gabriella pointed to Ryan. "We were busy getting schooled."

Ryan grinned at the compliment, but Troy looked confused – and felt a little left out.

Just then, Mr Fulton appeared in that sudden, spooky way of his and tapped on his watch. "Pool not quite ready, Miss Montez? We open in five minutes." He gestured towards Troy. "Mr Bolton, I think you're due on the golf course."

Troy headed for the clubhouse as Gabriella, sighing, went back to work.

The guys were in the staff changing room putting on their uniforms when Troy came in.

"Hey, how'd it go with the Redhawks?" Zeke called out.

"They're very . . . tall," Troy said. That seemed to sum up his first practise session with college guys as much as anything.

"We got Vince from maintenance to play," Zeke said. He didn't want Troy to forget that he'd let them down. Again. "So it worked out."

"Maybe we'll play later today," Troy said.

But his friends had already heard too many empty promises.

"Check with Vince," Chad said coolly.

Troy was starting to get annoyed. They were acting as if this was all his fault. Did they want

him to turn down a golden opportunity to practise with the Redhawks just so he could play softball? "Mr Evans set up the workout, not me," he
pointed out.

Chad wasn't going to let him off that easily.
"You ask to include us? Or maybe you ran out of
room on your 'to-do' list."

Now Troy was more than annoyed. He was
furious. "I didn't go looking for the Redhawks;
they came to me. I didn't sign up for this golf job;
Fulton offered it. But I said yes. My choice.
Because it's fun, and it's stuff I should be doing
for my future. I show up to work, same as you."

Chad had to roll his eyes at that last one. "Oh,
please, if you get a speck of dirt on your pants,
someone dry cleans you. You order off the menu,
we eat what's left."

Troy said hotly, "You'd be doing the same
thing, if . . ." He stopped, just a little bit too late.

". . . if we were as good as you?" Chad filled in
the rest.

"I didn't say that." But Troy knew he almost had.

"We voted you captain of the Wildcats not because you've got a good jump shot, but because you're the guy who's supposed to know what's up," Chad said. He added bitterly, "That was before the summer, though, wasn't it?"

"You think you've got me all figured out?" Troy said. "I don't think so."

Just then, Mr Fulton came in, took a look around, and said, "Gentlemen, you're not being paid to play Dr Phil. Recess is over. Get busy." He turned to Troy. "Bolton, Mr Evans wants you to meet him over at Indian Hills Country Club to golf with a couple of his business partners. He left you the keys to his Ferrari."

He handed Troy the keys, and Troy left without bothering to say goodbye.

The other Wildcats looked at each other.

"Ferrari?" Jason repeated. "All right, I admit it. Troy's a superior being."

"Yeah," Chad muttered. "Just ask him."

CHAPTER ELEVEN

For the next few days, all the Wildcats were busy, busy, busy.

Troy played more golf games with Mr Evans and the other Redhawks boosters. They listened to his golf tips, slapped him on the back when he made a great shot and treated him to fabulous dinners at the country club. This was definitely the good life, and Troy couldn't help loving it.

Ryan had a blast rehearsing the Wildcats dance number for the talent show – and they were surprised to find that they were having an awesome time working with him. Of course, they couldn't let Sharpay know what they were doing! Fortunately, she was busy rehearsing with Troy and Kelsi, organizing the show and trying not to wince when she saw some of the other talent that was going to take the stage.

Zeke kept creating new and better gourmet treats in the kitchen. And when Mr Fulton had a bite, he was quietly stunned by how good the food was. When they weren't working, the Wildcats still had fun – but Gabriella sometimes found herself looking for Troy, and feeling sad when he wasn't there.

Troy kept playing in the Redhawks' practise sessions. He was loving every minute of his introduction to college ball – but he did feel let down when he went to the kitchen to find his friends, only to discover that it was empty. And even though it was great to be out on the golf course, it didn't seem quite as much fun now that he never saw his friends.

But that was the way the summer was turning

out. Troy and the Wildcats now lived in two separate worlds.

A few days before the talent show, a crew arrived to put up a party tent. Troy arrived at the country club and walked over to take a look.

Crew members were rigging lighting, putting up sets, checking sound equipment. Troy's jaw dropped in amazement. This wasn't some little pup tent – it was a showcase!

Sharpay was looking at the seating chart with her mother. When she saw Troy, she waved him over and pointed to a table that was highlighted in red marker. "Daddy will make certain the entire scholarship committee is right here," she said. "Perfect view."

"And I've invited your parents as our guests," her mother said. "It'll be a grand evening."

Troy looked around at the huge tent, the massive stage, the lighting, the decorations, the whole luxurious, over-the-top atmosphere. Then he looked at Sharpay, who was dressed as if she belonged in the pages of a fashion magazine. He had to admit it: Sharpay and the life she lived had a lot going for it.

Sharpay led him onto the stage. As Kelsi began to play, Martha and Taylor poked their heads into the tent.

And suddenly, like it or not, Troy was singing a duet with Sharpay.

It was the music that had been written for him and Gabriella, but Sharpay's changes had made it something completely different. When he sang the duet with Gabriella, the music had seemed beautiful and emotional. Now, it was a Broadway-style extravaganza.

He did his best to sing the way he knew Sharpay wanted him to, but his heart wasn't in it. In fact, he felt as if he were trapped in a nightmare – and had no way out!

"Good thing there isn't a panel of judges," Martha said, watching him struggle.

Taylor nodded. "My sister's boy rule number seven: when boys mess up . . . they *really* go all out."

Finally, the song ended. Sharpay took Troy's hands and looked deep into his eyes. "You know, Troy, I've always known you were special. And it's pretty obvious that I'm special. I think we were meant to sing together, don't you? I'm so excited for your future, it's just all worked out like a dream come true."

But when he looked back at her, he saw her wearing a lavish wedding gown and holding a bouquet!

He could hardly speak. He was terrified.

"Troy?" Sharpay said.

"I need some air," he said quickly.

As he headed for the door, she called after him, "Don't be long, we need to run it again!"

Once Troy was outside, he ran off. He didn't stop until he got to the place where he always felt happy and in control: the basketball court. He grabbed a basketball and started taking shots. After a few minutes, he stopped in frustration. He couldn't help but notice that most of his shots were clunkers.

Then he heard something. Music and laughter . . . coming from the exercise room . . .

Sharpay was getting annoyed. Troy had run out of the door as if he were escaping something, and now, at least three – she checked her watch, no, *five* – minutes had gone by, and he still wasn't back.

She marched out of the clubhouse to look for him. As she walked past the pool, she saw shadows coming from the members' gym. She walked over to peer through the windows . . . and gasped as she saw the Wildcats rehearsing a dance number directed by her very own brother!

Scowling, Sharpay watched as these . . . these *nobodies* danced and sang and laughed. What Sharpay didn't see was that Troy was looking through the windows on the other side of the gym, thinking wistfully that his friends seemed to be having a great time. And that Gabriella looked beautiful . . .

* * *

When the rehearsal was over, the Wildcats left the gym after a few last hugs and jokes. Ryan stayed behind to collect his rehearsal notes and the CDs and boombox he'd been using. He was just about to head for home himself when the door swung open and Sharpay stormed in.

"I said keep an eye on them, not turn them into the Pussycat Dolls!" she yelled.

He grinned. "Pretty cool, huh?"

Sharpay was so astonished, she could barely breathe. "What are you doing to my show?! Do you want me to lose the Star Dazzle award to a bunch of . . . dishwashers?"

Ryan lifted his chin defiantly. "Your show? I'm part of a different show now, remember?"

"When did you become . . . one of them?" she demanded.

"Hey, that's a compliment," he said. "But you have a good show, Sis."

"Oh, I plan to," Sharpay said to herself as he walked away.

CHAPTER TWELVE

Sharpay went straight to Mr Fulton's office. "The Midsummer Night's Star Dazzle Talent Show means something to me, and to my family," she said. "Those Wildcats will turn it into one great big farce."

"Your brother is one of 'those Wildcats', I'm told," he countered.

"Don't mention that traitor to me," she snapped.

"Employee involvement in the Star Dazzle show is tradition," he pointed out.

"Traditions change," she said, dismissively. "My parents have important guests coming. We'll need every employee on duty that night, and not on the stage."

Mr Fulton hesitated. "You might want to think this one out."

"All right." Sharpay paused for a nanosecond, then said, "Done. Now do it." She stormed out of the office, feeling slightly happier.

Mr Fulton caught sight of himself in a mirror. "What are *you* looking at?" he said guiltily.

The next day, Mr Fulton handed Taylor a stack of memos. "Distribute these in the staff area," he ordered, "but not until end of shift."

"Of course," she said. Then she read the memo. "What?! Wait! But . . ."

"No discussion, Miss McKessie," Mr Fulton said. "This is a business. I'm sorry to be the one to tell you, but welcome to the world of adults who have jobs they wish to keep because they have mortgages they wish to pay . . . tuition bills, car payments, etc. So sometimes there are tasks, however unpleasant, required by employers in order for the aforementioned and all-important pay cheque to arrive in your all-too-empty pocket!"

After a moment, Taylor said quietly, "May I get you a cup of tea, Mr Fulton?"

"That would be lovely, thank you," he replied.

A short time later, a glum group of Wildcats were gathered in the kitchen.

"How are we supposed to do a show if we've got a full shift?" Martha asked.

"I think that's the point," Taylor said.

Gabriella entered the kitchen, and Taylor handed her a memo. "Nothing we can do. Fulton's orders," Taylor explained.

Chad snorted at that. "No way this is Fulton's idea, unless Fulton suddenly has blonde hair and wears designer dresses."

Gabriella finished the memo, her eyes wide. But she wasn't just upset. She was angry.

* * *

Sharpay was packing her pool bag when Gabriella stormed over to her.

"Forget about the rest of us, how about the fact that your brother has worked incredibly hard on this show?" she said heatedly.

"Oh, boo-hoo." Sharpay shrugged. "He'll be in the show. He's a member. And don't lecture me about Ryan, given the way you've been interfering with Troy's future."

Gabriella's mouth fell open. "What?"

"You've got him written up by Mr Fulton for sneaking onto the golf course, swimming after hours . . ." Sharpay pointed out. "I had to step in just to save Troy's job. He is worried about his future, worried about college, and all I've tried to do is help."

"What's that got to do with messing with our show?" Gabriella asked.

Sharpay glared at her. "You recruited Ryan because you're jealous of what I've done for Troy."

"I'm not talking about Troy," Gabriella said,

frustrated. "I'm talking about my friends, your brother, my summer."

Sharpay rolled her eyes. "Oh, please. You don't like the fact that I won."

"What's the prize? Troy? The Star Dazzle award? You have to go through all this to get either one?" Gabriella yelled. "No thanks, Sharpay. You're very good at a game I don't even want to be a part of. Your club, your world, and you're welcome to it. But just step away from the mirror long enough to see who gets hurt when you win."

I could respond to that, Sharpay thought, I simply choose not to. So, instead, she grabbed her bag and stalked away.

Troy entered the kitchen, hoping to find everybody still there. The room was empty except for Taylor, who was looking pretty upset.

She hadn't been too friendly to Troy lately, so he thought he'd say something light to brighten her mood. "If I have to teach one more junior clinic, I'm going to need a suit of armour."

"Might not be a bad idea," she said.

She handed him a memo. He read it, then said, "Oh, man . . . this is messed up."

"Like you didn't see it coming?" she asked.

He shot her a look. "What's that mean?"

"It's pretty obvious that big stage is just for you and your new best friend, Sharpay," she replied.

Troy's mind went immediately to the one person he did *not* want to think that. "Does Gabriella think that's what I want?"

Taylor shook her head. "Boyfriend rule number ten: wake up and smell the coffee, dude!"

"Where is she?" Troy asked.

Taylor shrugged. "Don't know. She told me this is her last day at Lava Springs."

"*What*?" Troy cried. He had to talk to her, he had to change her mind. He rushed outside and bounded down the steps, just catching Gabriella as she was packing her shoulder bag.

"You can't leave," he said breathlessly.

"Us working together sounded good, Troy, but things change. Right?" she said sadly.

"So give me a chance to make them change again," he said.

She gave him a serious look. "The talent show is a huge deal for Sharpay. It's a big deal for your future, too. That's cool."

He was shaking his head. She totally had the wrong idea, he had to set her straight . . . "The golf, the singing, I'm just trying to work out this scholarship thing."

"Except when I talk to you, I don't know who I'm talking to any more."

Troy felt a chill. "It's me."

A spark of anger appeared in Gabriella's eyes. "Blowing off your friends, missing dates? If that's you, it's good to know."

"I just need to get through this show," he explained.

"All I know is if you act like someone you're not, then pretty soon that's who you become," she said.

Troy stopped. He was afraid, deep down inside, that she was right.

"When I said I haven't had a summer in one place for five years, that was the truth," she said. "I want it to be special, and this isn't the place for that to happen."

A little desperately, he said, "I meant what I said about movies, skateboarding and being together."

"I'm sure you did," she said coolly. "At the time."

"I'm just trying to catch up with it all."

She nodded. "Me, too. Because summer's happening, and I'm going to go find it. But I'll see you in September."

Fighting back tears, she walked into the kitchen and began to empty her locker. She remembered how much she'd looked forward to a summer with all her new friends . . . and Troy. She knew that it wouldn't do any good to stay in this job, hoping that the summer would end up the way she had planned. No, she had to go her own way and make sure she had a summer she'd never forget.

When she left the kitchen, Troy was waiting. She knew that he had his own path to follow as well, and she couldn't really blame him.

A car honked. She looked at Troy. "Gotta go."

As she walked to the car park, three people watched her leave, all feeling different emotions.

Troy felt confused and sad. He had messed everything up and he wasn't sure how to fix it.

Taylor felt angry with Troy and upset to see Gabriella go.

And Sharpay felt nothing but a deep satisfaction. Everything, she thought, is working out *perfectly*.

That night, Troy was sitting alone in his room when there was a knock on the door. His dad came in, holding a plate of ribs.

"Usually you're taking these right off the grill," he said. He could see that his son was upset about something.

Troy shrugged. "Maybe I've been eating too much at the club."

His dad tried again. "Thought you'd be inviting the guys over for these ribs. I bought a couple of extra slabs."

Troy hesitated, then said, "Do you think I seem real . . . different to you, dad?"

"You dress a lot better than usual," Mr Bolton said, trying to lighten the mood a bit. He looked at Troy more seriously. "What's up?"

"Gabriella is quitting because she thinks I'm going overboard working the scholarship thing. I'm just doing the show with Sharpay because she's hooked me up with the boosters and all that. I don't really care about the golf, and playing with the Redhawks is cool but not if my guys don't even want to come over here and play hoops any more," Troy said in a rush.

"Whoa . . . whoa," his dad said. "Troy, I hope you're only doing that talent show because you want to do it."

Want to do it? Troy thought he *had* to do it! "I get it that hanging with Mr Evans and the boosters is a really big deal for my future," he said cautiously.

His dad sat down on the bed. Clearly, it was time to set the record straight. "I got carried away talking up shaking hands at Lava Springs. But whatever college turns out to be right for you, scholarship or not, we'll make it work as a family. We've got your back, Troy."

"Yeah?" Troy said, feeling the first ray of hope that he had felt since . . . since Sharpay had started micro-managing his life.

"Bet on it," his dad said. "Here's my only rule about the future: wherever you go, just make sure you don't leave yourself behind."

Troy smiled at his dad as a huge wave of relief swept through his body.

But when Troy arrived at work the next day, the first thing he noticed was that there was a new lifeguard on duty. And when he walked through the kitchen, he could sense that his friends were uneasy around him.

As the day wore on, it was clear that the only one having fun was Sharpay.

Kelsi played the piano for the lunch crowd without her usual sparkle. Ryan sat by the pool, but even the beautiful day couldn't cheer him up. Taylor walked through the kitchen and noticed how quiet it was.

And Troy just waited for the day to end. Everyone, he knew, was missing Gabriella . . . but nobody missed her more than he did.

Finally, the day was over. Troy hopped in a golf cart and didn't stop until he got to the middle of the empty course. He took several deep breaths of the night air, stuck a tee in the ground, picked up a golf club, and swung.

The ball sailed through the twilight. Troy watched it go, wondering what had happened to his carefree summer. He thought about how he had fallen in with other people's plans for his future without considering what he wanted to do. And then he made a very important decision.

Things were about to change. From now on, Troy Bolton was going to chart his own course.

CHAPTER THIRTEEN

The next morning started out just like any other at Lava Springs Country Club. Club members ate breakfast on the terrace, golfers walked out to the range and tennis players warmed up their serves.

On the 18th hole, a man hunched over his golf club, preparing to make a short putt. But just as he drew the club back to hit the ball, the air was torn by a piercing scream. "WHAT?!!!"

The golfer flinched, knocking his ball off the green.

A tennis player hit her serve into the fence.

In the kitchen, a chef tossed an omelette completely out of the pan.

A diver's beautiful jackknife turned into a clumsy belly flop.

A valet backed a car into a sign advertising the talent show, knocking the sign to the ground.

And on the stage inside the party tent, Sharpay was hyperventilating as Troy stood by.

"What do you mean you're not going to be in my show?" she cried in outraged tones.

"That's exactly it," he said calmly.

Could it be that he just didn't understand the enormity of what he was saying? "We're singing a *duet*, Troy," she explained impatiently. "A duet means two people. Mostly me in this case, but whatever. Duet."

He shrugged. "I'm an employee, and there aren't any employees in the show."

"You're an honorary member," she explained.

"Was," Troy said. "I'm asking Mr Fulton for my kitchen job back. The memo said they're shorthanded on staff for the party."

"Listen to me, there's too much at stake for you tonight," she said impatiently. "An entire table of university boosters are all coming to see *you*. Thanks to me."

"Too bad they're going to miss Ryan and the Wildcats," Troy said. "That's worth seeing."

"They're not messing up my show!" she snapped.

"Then neither am I," he said firmly.

"But your parents are coming, too!" she wailed.

"I'll be their waiter," he said. "They'll be thrilled." He turned on his heel and walked off.

Kelsi had watched the whole scene from a corner of the room. Now she watched Troy go, her eyes wide. And Sharpay – Kelsi had never seen her so angry!

She didn't know what this meant, except that it was sure to be a wild night!

That evening, there was a festive air at Lava

Springs Country Club as a crowd of members, all dressed in their best, filled the party tent. Chatting happily, they sat down at balloon-decked tables to eat their lavish dinners.

Backstage, Sharpay was dressed in her costume, trying to make Mr Fulton see things her way. For once, this wasn't working.

"I cannot order Mr Bolton to sing," the manager said. "That's not part of his job description." He adjusted the tuxedo he was wearing and added hopefully, "However, as you know I do have a theatrical background, and I think I can still hit a high C, if asked in a pinch . . ."

"I don't need a high C, I need divine intervention," she snapped. "We have 300 people arriving." She turned to the club girls. "I thought I told Lea to find Ryan!"

"She did," Ryan said. "Here I am."

"Thank goodness," Sharpay said. "Warm up the volcano. 'Humu Humu' is back in."

"Enjoy your pineapple on your own, Sharpay," Ryan said. "I'm not doing the show."

"What?!" Sharpay gasped. Was *everyone* turning against her? "Get your costume on."

But Ryan shook his head. "I took your advice. I sold it on eBay. You love the spotlight. Guess what? Now it's all yours."

He turned and left, happy to have had – for once – the last word.

Troy hung his golf clothes, carefully wrapped in plastic bags, in his staff locker. He put his golf clubs away. He placed the golf-cart key on the shelf. Then he pulled his name badge off the locker and buttoned his waiter's jacket, ready to go to work.

When he turned around, he found Chad, Zeke, Jason and Ryan standing behind him with their arms folded.

"Kelsi told us what went down between you and Sharpay," Chad said.

Troy sensed an opening, a chance to make things right with his friends, and he decided to take it. "I'm sorry I messed up your show."

"Yeah, and show business is our entire lives," Zeke said with a grin.

Troy laughed. "I know I've been acting pretty weird. I'm hoping you haven't permanently filled my slot in the two-on-two game. And, Ryan, I know you put a lot of work in with these guys . . . so I apologize."

The guys nodded. All they had wanted was an apology . . . and their old friend Troy back.

"We think you should sing tonight," Chad said.

"What? I already made up my mind," Troy replied.

"All those people are out there," Ryan said persuasively. "You're good. And I don't really want to see my sister crash and burn." He stopped and thought. "At least, I think I don't." He turned to Zeke. "By the way, I hope you hid that pastry trolley because when Sharpay gets nervous, she eats."

Sharpay was, in fact, very nervous. She had the pastry trolley in her dressing room and was stuffing one dessert after another into her mouth when Mr Fulton came in.

"I don't want to tell you how to produce your show, but the first three acts haven't exactly lit the house on fire," he said.

"I'm ruined," she said through a mouthful of éclair. "My life is over! I've been a good girl. I've never lied, except when necessary. I've always bought my parents expensive gifts – using their credit card, of course. But I don't deserve this humiliation . . ."

Mr Fulton decided it was time to interrupt this aria of self-pity. "At the very least, you'd better get out there and sing. It's either you or Mrs Hoffenfeffer and her talking sock puppet."

"Take me now, God," Sharpay said.

"I think I remember my old soft shoe," Mr Fulton said eagerly. "I'll give it a try. But you better warm up those vocal cords."

He left, and Sharpay slumped in front of her dressing-room mirror. She caught sight of her reflection: her hair was a mess, her face was smeared with frosting and, worst of all, she looked like what she was: a girl who had manipulated everyone to get what she wanted.

"What would Madonna do in this situation?" she asked herself. After a moment's thought, she said, "Okay, forget that."

As she stared bleakly into the mirror, she saw Troy reflected behind her. She whirled around.

"How's your show going?" he asked.

"How's it going?" She sighed and admitted, "My show makes the captain of the Titanic look like he won the lottery."

He hesitated, then said, "I'll sing with you, Sharpay."

She stared at him, incredulous. "What?"

"I did promise to sing with you, and I keep my promises," he explained. "But what was that thing you said to me when I first started working here?"

She cast her mind back. "Bring me an iced tea?"

He smiled a little. "Think harder." He prompted her, "We're . . ."

She paused, then said, ". . . all in this together."

"Yeah, that." Troy waited for her to connect the dots.

"Well . . . we are, so let's get out there and knock 'em dead, Troy Bolton!" she said brightly.

He sighed as he realized that he was going to have to explain this. "But not just you and me, Sharpay. The Wildcats, too. I do the show . . . if the Wildcats do the show." He glanced over at the demolished slices of cheesecake, coconut cake and apple torte. "Or do you just want to sit here and polish off what's left of the pastry trolley?"

Outside the door, Kelsi was listening intently.

Sharpay thought about the mess of a show that was happening right now onstage. She looked at the mirror and saw the mess she had become. And then she looked at Troy.

"I just sort of wish you were doing this . . . for me," she said, sincere for the first time. "You're a good guy, Troy . . . Actually, right now I think I like you better than I like myself." Startled, she looked at him with wide eyes. "Did I say that?"

He grinned, realizing for the first time that maybe Sharpay was someone he could actually be friends with.

CHAPTER FOURTEEN

Word spread through the Wildcats' ranks that they were going to be in the show! Chad jumped on a trolley and flew backstage, picking Taylor up on the way. Jason and Kelsi came running out of the kitchen, with Zeke right behind them.

Ryan grabbed Troy as he ran by and said, "Sharpay wants to do a different song. Kelsi will work it out with you."

"What? But . . . ." Troy was already nervous, and now he was supposed to sing a completely different song?

130

Ryan nodded reassuringly. "Just go with it."

"Where's Chad and Taylor?" Troy asked.

Kelsi grabbed Troy and pulled him to her piano to practise. They didn't have time for Troy to be nervous or to ask questions, she thought. After all, they didn't want to spoil the surprise . . .

While the excitement was building at the country club, Gabriella was lying on her bed reading a book.

Suddenly, Chad and Taylor burst into her room. Taylor went to her wardrobe and began pulling out dresses.

Gabriella sat up, shocked. "What are you—"

"Yell at us in the car," Chad said briefly.

She shook her head, confused. "Why aren't you working?"

Taylor grinned at her. "We are."

Gabriella's lips tightened. "I'm not going back to the club," she said firmly.

"Explain that to Ryan," Taylor suggested.

"Our show's back in, and he said nothing will work without you. Trust me, he's right."

Gabriella hesitated. Taylor and Chad exchanged a look of satisfaction.

Gabriella was in.

A magician was onstage, performing his tricks.

Troy's parents watched the act with a mixture of amazement and dismay as they ate their dinner.

"What do you think?" Mr Bolton asked.

"Well . . . it's nothing I've ever seen before," his wife said.

"Keep smiling," he replied.

She rolled her eyes. "That's the easy part."

While Sharpay sat backstage doing vocal exercises, Mr Fulton took the microphone.

"And now, ladies and gentlemen, I've been handed a change in the programme," he said. "I'm not quite sure what to expect, but, as they say, the show must go on . . ."

Kelsi ran onstage to sit at the piano while a flurry of activity went on in the wings.

"Why'd you switch songs?" Troy asked Sharpay. "I don't know if I can pull this off."

She looked at him with an expression of shocked surprise. "Switched songs? WHAT?"

He met her look with one of confusion. "Yeah. Ryan said . . ."

Onstage, Mr Fulton was saying, "So, here's our assistant golf pro, Troy Bolton . . ."

Kelsi began playing. Troy gulped, but he went onstage and began singing.

Sharpay spotted Ryan. "How am I supposed to get through this?" she asked. "I don't know this song."

"I know," he said simply.

She looked at him for a puzzled moment, then realized what was happening just as the back curtain opened to reveal all the Wildcats. They moved aside and Gabriella stepped onto the stage, singing along with Troy.

And here they were, back where they had

started . . . Troy and Gabriella, singing for a roomful of people but with eyes only for each other. They performed the song sweetly and simply and, as it gradually built to the finish, it seemed clear that this was a song about two voices that were meant to be together.

When they finished, there was a moment of silence, then the ballroom burst into applause. Troy hugged Gabriella.

Caught up in the spirit of the evening, Sharpay grabbed the microphone and introduced Ryan and the Wildcats. Ryan cued Kelsi, who began playing – and before anyone could blink, the Wildcats had turned the entire ballroom into their stage! They were singing about being friends and believing in each other. And when the song ended, the entire room erupted into a huge celebration!

In the midst of it all, Troy's dad found him and said, "I thought you told me you weren't having fun here. Could have fooled me."

Troy grinned, but before he could reply,

Sharpay's dad came up to them. "I've been talking to the committee," he said. "It's pretty much unanimous. Doesn't matter what happens on court next year. We want Troy at U of A whatever. Just the kind of kid we want on campus."

Troy's mouth dropped open. It was beyond anything he had dreamed of – but it was happening awfully fast . . . and he didn't know what to say.

"Well, Troy will need to think about his options," Mr Bolton said easily, rescuing him. "Too early to tell. Summer's just starting."

Troy glanced at his dad and smiled. There would be time enough to think about the future – *after* he'd had the best summer ever.

Then Mr Fulton stepped back onstage, holding the Star Dazzle award.

"Ladies and gentlemen, the winner of this year's Star Dazzle award is, of course, our one and only–"

Before he could finish, Sharpay grabbed the

microphone and said, "Mr Ryan Evans!"

She took the award from Mr Fulton and handed it to a shocked but beaming Ryan, then she turned to find that Zeke was standing in front of her and holding out a pastry.

"Chocolate éclair?" she cried. "How did you know that was my favourite?"

"Wild guess," he grinned. "Maybe it was the three you ate before the show? But there are more on the way."

It had been a night to remember – and the fun only continued the next day, when the club was closed for an employees-only party. Everyone – including Sharpay! – hung out at the pool. They even sang and danced a little.

Later that night, the Wildcats were lying on the golf course, enjoying the afterglow of their triumph.

"Man, what a party!" Troy exclaimed.

"Glad we don't have to clean it up," Chad said.

"Actually," Taylor said, "I think we do."

Gabriella smiled dreamily. "But not until tomorrow."

Zeke nodded. "When we're back on the clock and getting paid," he added pointedly.

After a small pause, Sharpay said, "I'll help."

Every head snapped in her direction. Everyone was shocked – but no one was more shocked than Sharpay.

"Did I say that?" she asked.

Suddenly, the sprinklers all began spraying water everywhere. There were joyous shrieks as the Wildcats got thoroughly soaked. They started racing across the grass, laughing.

But Troy and Gabriella hung back a little, and gazed at each other. It felt as if everything was right again. Caught up in the moment, they leaned in and at last they kissed tenderly. The night couldn't have been more perfect. Smiling at each other, they ran after their friends under the starry summer sky.

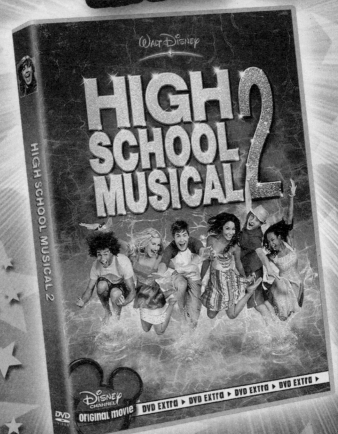

BOPPING BACK ON TO Disney DVD XMAS '07

Walt Disney

HIGH SCHOOL MUSICAL 2

HIGH SCHOOL MUSICAL 2

Disney CHANNEL ORIGINAL MOVIE

DVD EXTra ▸ DVD EXTra ▸ DVD EXTra ▸ DVD EXTra ▸

ROLL ON SUMMER!

Although I was nervous transferring to East High, it turned out to be a great year and I was really excited about spending the summer with all of my new friends. For once, I wasn't moving somewhere new, and when I learned that we were all going to work together at the Lava Springs Club, I just couldn't wait for the summer to start. Building friendships, making extra cash for college and most importantly, spending a lot more time with Troy. However, the summer didn't turn out quite the way I imagined...

★ SHARPAY'S SECRET DIARY ★

Sharpay is always trying to get her drama-queen clutches on Troy Bolton, East High's 'Primo Boy' and these secret diary entries reveal just how far she'll go.

Thursday

Mercifully, summer vacation is almost here. This year did not turn out the way I expected, at all. First, Gabriella sweeps in from nowhere and had the absolute gall to steal the lead in the Winter Musical that by all rights should have been mine (and would have, too, if Ms Darbus hadn't begun to slip a little, poor woman). However, this summer will bring me sweet redemption. As soon as the Lava Springs talent competition gets underway, nobody will have any doubt that the most fabulously talented person in the show is yours truly.

Friday

My plan was so simple a ten year old could have carried it out! Lure Troy to Lava Springs. Not Troy and his cronies, and definitely NOT GABRIELLA!! And yet the usually capable and obedient Mr Fulton managed to mess the whole thing up. Half of East High is here, and not only that, but Fulton and my mother are going to sit back and let it happen. Well, if I have to do everything myself, fine, at least I know it will get done right. Hmmmm... I just heard that the tiny traitor Kelsi wrote a song just for Troy and Gabriella. This would have infuriated me if it hadn't inspired me first! Troy will sing a duet at the talent show, but it won't be with that upstart Gabriella. It will be with me!

You decide how cool the East High Wildcats really are. Read the profiles and score each personality trait out of 10, then add up the scores to see who's hot and who's not!

TROY:

1. Great natural singer
2. Amazing basketball player
3. Sincere and caring
4. Tries to do the right thing
5. Sometimes worries too much about what other people think or expect from him

TOTAL

CHAD:

1. Extremely loyal to his friends
2. Totally dedicated to basketball
3. Willing to put in hard work to try to impress a girl
4. Sometimes has a chip on his shoulder
5. Can be a little quick to judge (singing, dancing, cooking and pretty much any non-basketball related pursuit!)

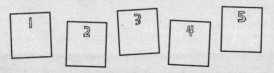

TOTAL

ZEKE:

1. Good basketball player
2. Really cares about his friends
3. Goofy sense of humour
4. Bakes, if that helps
5. Likes Sharpay!

TOTAL

1 2 3 4 5

RYAN:

1. Dedicated to his family (especially his sister!)
2. Good singer
3. Has a good eye for talent
4. Comes into his own when he steps outside his sister's shadow
5. Somewhat vain

TOTAL

1 2 3 4 5

ABOUT THE BOYS

What do you think the girls of East High really think of the wild Wildcat boys? Now's your chance to decide! Fill in the thought bubbles below to reveal what the girls secretly think of the boys!

Troy's the captain of the basketball team, but has discovered that he also enjoys the thrills of the theatre. What do the East High girls make of his split priorities?

Chad is straightforward and to-the-point. You know where you are with this basketball-obsessed boy. But does he appeal to the girls?

Ryan is often overshadowed by his flamboyant sister, but behind the Sharpay side-kick, there is a caring and talented young man. What do the girls of East High make of this show-stopper?

A DAY IN THE LIFE OF TROY BOLTON

Being the Primo Boy of East High is hard work. Barely an hour goes by when he isn't fending off the advances of a loved-up girl. Check out an hour by hour schedule of Troy's busy day at Lava Springs.

8:00: Clock in

8:15: Try to steal a few minutes with Gabriella before having to get down to work

8:16: Caught and told off by Mr Fulton - it's a good thing this country club doesn't have detention!

8:17: Prepare silverware for days' dining. Can never seem to get these stupid linen napkins folded right...

8:30: 'Sweep the perimeter' of dining room and make sure everything is clean and ready. Sweep floors, set tables, more folding (ugghh!), put food on trolleys.

9:00-10:30: Wait tables for breakfast and brunch and brunch rushes. Load and empty dishwashers when traffic is light. More table setting, napkin folding (will it never end?!), water bearing, order taking. Running back and forth to poolside to wait on club members. Try to avoid Sharpay and her stable of manicured friends. Probably unsuccessful, since she seems to be just about everywhere. I can't help bumping in to her.

10:30: Told to suit up and caddie.

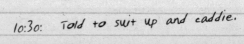

10:35: Discovered that I was caddying for Sharpay and her family. (Didn't see that coming.)

11:00: Snuck over to pool in between holes and made plans with Gabriella for lunch.

11:50: Playing golf with the Evans family wasn't as bad as I thought it might be. I actually kind of enjoyed myself.

12:00: Tried to clock out to meet Gabriella, but Mr Evans insisted I talk to him instead. (I'll have to make it up to her later.)

13:00-14:00:
Lunch rush. (They aren't kidding about the rush part! This place makes basketball practice look easy!)

14:00-15:00: Cleanup duty. (It doesn't get any better than this!)

15:00-16:00: Preparations for dinner rush. (Man, there are a lot of preparations going on around this place!)

16:00-17:00: Serve dinner. To be followed by, of course...

17:00-18:00: Surprise, surprise! More cleanup!! Gabriella

18:15: Clean myself up and meet Gabriella for dinner. Try to make it up to her for missing lunch. Maybe we can even sneak in the pool tonight after everyone leaves. Then I have to try to get some rest tonight and gear up for the whole thing again tomorrow.

A DAY IN THE LIFE OF SHARPAY EVANS ★

Being a fabulous starlet-in-the-making takes a lot of organization. You'll never find Sharpay sitting around relaxing (sun bathing doesn't count – a tan is an integral part of her look). Check out an hour by hour schedule of Sharpay's busy day at Lava Springs.

8:00: Morning beauty routine – cleansing, toning, moisturizing, hair straightening and outfit selection.

9:00: Find out where Troy and Gabriella are and spy on them to discover what they're up to – having far too much fun, no doubt!

9:30: Give Fulton instructions to send more work Gabriella's way. Today the restaurant is serving sautéed potatoes and those potatoes won't peel themselves! Honestly, what's the point of a manager who needs managing?

10:00– Spa time. Aromatherapy massage, eyebrow pluck
11:30: and a long soak in the Jacuzzi. All this working, really takes it out of a girl!

11:35– Catch up with Ryan to find out if he's seen anything
12:30: of interest while following Troy and Gabriella.

12:40– Lunch on the terrace with Mum and Dad. Dad couldn't
13:45: stop talking about how he thinks Troy is such a promising young man. This could be useful...

TROY

14:00- Follow Troy as he caddies his way around the golf
15.30: course. He kept sneaking off to see Gabriella, who
still hasn't finished peeling those potatoes!

15:40: Discover the Wildcats messing around in
the kitchen instead of prepping for dinner.
Immediately tell Fulton to sort it out. We are
not paying these layabouts to have fun here!

15:50- Manage to find Troy alone (finally!) and suggest
16:00: how beneficial singing a duet with me could be for
him. He seemed intimidated by my fabulous natural
talent, but I think, if I can keep that upstart
Gabriella busy enough, Troy will come running to me!

16:10- Shopping for fabulous costume
17:30: accessories. I found an amazing sparkly
headdress that is simply stunning. But
not as stunning as me. Obviously.

17:45- Join Ryan for dinner, and make sure there is
18.30: plenty of clearing up for Gabriella to do once the
service time is over.

18:40- Follow Troy, only to find him heading back to the
19:00: kitchen to help Gabriella! Is there no separating
these two?

19:00: Have a relaxing bubble bath and apply face mask.
Spend the rest of the evening catching up on the
latest trends in this month's fashion magazines before
settling down to some much-needed beauty sleep.

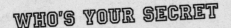

WHO'S YOUR SECRET CRUSH?

Take the quiz and find out which of East High's Wildcats you secretly fancy deep down – the results could be surprising!

1. WHAT IS YOUR IDEA OF A GREAT DATE?

   A. Going to a basketball game
   B. Going to a karaoke club
   C. A night in front of the TV with ice cream and fresh-baked cookies
   D. A trip the theatre

2. WHAT'S YOUR FAVOURITE COLOUR?

   A. Wildcat colours, all the way!
   B. It changes frequently and without warning
   C. Caramel. Or salmon. Or lime. Mmmm... is anyone else hungry?
   D. All colours look good on me

3. WHAT DO YOU LIKE TO DO WITH YOUR FREE TIME?

   A. Play sports
   B. I have a lot of interests: several sports, singing, hanging out with friends
   C. Cook, followed closely by eat
   D. See a good play or, better, yet, a musical

4. WHAT CHARACTER TRAIT DO YOU LOOK FOR MOST IN A PARTNER?

   A. Drive: know what you want and do anything to get it
   B. A spirit of adventure
   C. Gentleness and a kind heart
   D. Unwavering loyalty

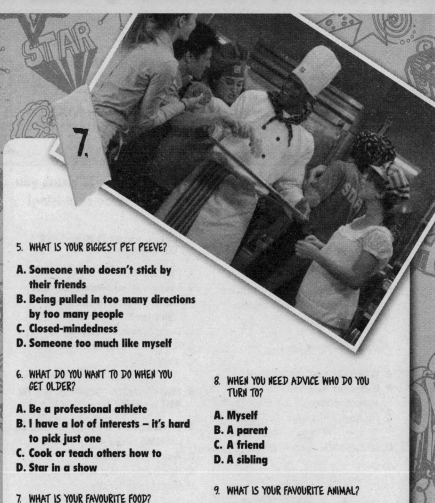

7.

5. WHAT IS YOUR BIGGEST PET PEEVE?

A. Someone who doesn't stick by
   their friends
B. Being pulled in too many directions
   by too many people
C. Closed-mindedness
D. Someone too much like myself

**6. WHAT DO YOU WANT TO DO WHEN YOU
   GET OLDER?**

A. Be a professional athlete
B. I have a lot of interests – it's hard
   to pick just one
C. Cook or teach others how to
D. Star in a show

7. WHAT IS YOUR FAVOURITE FOOD?

A. Pizza, burgers, whatever really...
   it's all just fuel
B. Homemade ribs
C. Sea bass. No, crème brulle. No,
   filet mignon. No...
D. Anything that looks as good as
   it tastes

**8. WHEN YOU NEED ADVICE WHO DO YOU
   TURN TO?**

A. Myself
B. A parent
C. A friend
D. A sibling

9. WHAT IS YOUR FAVOURITE ANIMAL?

A. Wildcat!
B. Wolf – they understand what it
   means to be part of a team
C. Bear – they really know how to eat
   and sleep!
D. Peacock

NOW TURN THE PAGE TO DISCOVER WHICH HIGH
SCHOOL MUSICAL HUNK IS YOUR SECRET CRUSH!

ANSWER KEY:

If you answered mostly:

As: You're made for a boy with mad skills and dedication like Chad.

Bs: You need someone whose variety and willingness to change can match your own, like Troy.

Cs: You're a Zeke freak. You like someone laid back, funny and good in the kitchen!

Ds: You value good fashion sense, some talent (but not too much!) and loyalty. Ryan would be the co-star in your stage show.